The next morning, Chris and Susan did something they didn't usually do.

They dressed exactly the same.

Deciding to make a point of being sisters—*twin* sisters, at that—had something to do with wanting to present a "united front" to B.J. Wilkins.

"This should impress him," Chris said with a satisfied nod. "Having him see us both looking like the same person should make him understand the seriousness of what he's done. Imagine, trying to violate the Twins' Code of Honor."

"The *what*?" asked Susan.

"It's something I just made up. But it sounds good, doesn't it?"

"Definitely. Very official. Well, even if we don't manage to impress him with how upset we both are about all this, we should at least manage to confuse him!"

THE PUMPKIN PRINCIPLE

Cynthia Blair

FAWCETT JUNIPER • NEW YORK

RLI: $\dfrac{\text{VL: 5 \& up}}{\text{IL: 6 \& up}}$

A Fawcett Juniper Book
Published by Ballantine Books
Copyright © 1986 by Cynthia Blair

Library of Congress Catalog Card Number: 86-91182

ISBN: 0-449-70205-7

First Edition: October 1986
Fourth Printing: June 1988

One

"I love autumn," said Christine Pratt with a dramatic sigh. "It's my favorite season. I always feel like something wonderful, something unbelievably *exciting*, is going to happen at any minute."

"I know exactly what you mean." Her twin sister, Susan, nodded in agreement. "Why, even the air smells different!" She threw back her head and took a deep breath.

Chris sniffed the air tentatively. "You're right," she said. "It's as if the air were . . . *crispy*. Like the leaves!"

The two girls laughed, partly because of Chris's colorful description of the brisk October morning, partly because each knew exactly what the other meant.

They were on their way to school, strolling down First Street toward Whittington High, where they were both just starting their senior year. Fortunately, it was one of those rare days when they both managed to be ready to leave the house right on time, so they could enjoy a leisurely walk.

And it was the perfect morning for such a stroll. The sky was a clear powder blue, the sun was bright, and the air was, indeed, crisp. It was the kind of day that always made both girls feel energetic.

Chris, in fact, was feeling particularly frisky.

"I think there's something magical about fall," she said, her dark brown eyes glowing mischievously. "After all, October is when Halloween is, right?"

"Well, yes, but that's just one day out of the whole season. What else is there that's magical?"

"Why, Susan Pratt! I'm surprised at you! Where's your imagination? Look around you. What do you see?"

Susan blinked, surprised by the fact that her twin was suddenly becoming so observant. Usually, she was the practical, down-to-earth one, while Chris ran around with her head in the clouds. Dutifully, she looked around.

"I see beautiful leaves—red and orange and yellow. A few clouds in the sky that look like cotton balls. And the sun looks like it's trying as hard as it possibly can. I guess all that's pretty magical, isn't it?"

"Yes, but there's even more. What else do you see? Come on, Sooz. It's something you don't see any other time of the year. *Ever!*"

"Do I get a clue?" Susan was beginning to get impatient with her sister's teasing—and her mysteriousness.

"Okay, just one. Take a look up ahead at the Petersons' house."

Susan turned to look at the house belonging to the elderly couple who ran Whittington's bookstore. It was a pleasant, white shingled building, plain but well cared for. There were flowers planted in front, a new coat of paint on the low fence that surrounded the property . . . and three huge pumpkins sitting on the porch.

"Pumpkins!" Susan squealed. "Of course. I should have

2

guessed right away." She turned to her twin, her eyes wide. "Chris, do you think pumpkins have magical powers?"

Chris was suddenly matter-of-fact. "Well, *of course,* Sooz. Do you know of any other fruit that gets picked, goes into people's houses—and then emerges a few days later with a *face*?"

"You've got a point there." Her sister laughed. "But do you think there's any more to it than that? After all, Cinderella's pumpkin turned into a coach."

"That was not your ordinary pumpkin. After all, you were dealing with a fairy godmother there. No, I'm not talking about that. I'm talking about your basic, everyday, run-of-the-mill pumpkin. Like the ones on the Petersons' porch."

"Gee, those pumpkins don't even have faces yet."

"Doesn't matter. You see, I've developed a theory." Chris continued in the same mock-serious tone.

"A theory?"

"Right. I've given this a lot of thought. And I've developed what I call the Pumpkin Principle. It's the result of years of research. And personal observation, too, of course. Yes, I've examined the issue closely."

"That sounds terribly scientific," her sister returned. "Tell me, Dr. Pratt, precisely what *is* the Pumpkin Principle?"

"I've come to the conclusion that pumpkins have mysterious, magical powers. Whenever they appear—usually every autumn—they give people an overwhelming urge to . . ."

"To *what*?" Susan was so caught up in her twin's little fantasy that she almost dropped the pile of schoolbooks she was carrying.

"To pretend to be someone other than themselves." Chris

3

turned to Susan, wearing a smug expression. "See? As I said, I've given the Pumpkin Principle a lot of thought."

"Wait a minute. I'm not sure I understand. What do you mean, 'pretend to be someone other than themselves'?"

Christine shrugged. "Dressing up, wearing masks and costumes and disguises, taking on other identities . . . it's all part of the same syndrome. People just become overwhelmed with this—this *need*. I tell you, it's the pumpkins. There's something about their very presence."

"You must be right. After all," Susan said with feigned innocence, "I don't know *anybody* who would *ever* pretend to be somebody else unless it was Halloween. Do you?"

She and Chris burst out laughing, for on several occasions, the Pratt sisters, identical twins, had done just that. They had tried switching identities for two whole weeks once, Chris pretending to be Susan and vice versa, so that each could learn more about what her twin's life was like. They had nicknamed that caper the Banana Split Affair, since they had bet each other whether it would work or not and the stakes had been the biggest banana split they could find.

Then, when Chris had been awarded the honor of being selected the honorary "queen" of Whittington, the girls' hometown, during its week-long celebration of its hundred-year anniversary, the twins had taken turns filling the role, since they had worked together on the research project that won Chris that honor. That time, they had had fewer doubts that they could pull it off—and they had decided to celebrate, at the end of the festivities, with hot fudge sundaes at Fozzy's, Whittington's brand-new ice cream parlor. That little adventure had been dubbed the Hot Fudge Sunday Affair. And later that same summer—one that they came to call "Strawberry Summer"—even though the twins had vowed not to try to pull off any more pranks while working as camp counselors at Camp Pinewood, the fact that they were identical had helped them fool someone at a crucial moment—and save the camp from being forced to close down.

The Pratt twins looked enough alike to fool their girlfriends, their dates, even their parents. They both had dark brown eyes and shoulder-length chestnut hair, and their features were identical, including impish ski-jump noses and high cheekbones.

But their similarities ended there. Chris was outgoing and talkative. She loved her busy life, participating in school clubs, keeping up with the latest fads in clothes and records, and juggling a busy social schedule. Susan, meanwhile, was much quieter, preferring to spend as much time as she could reading and working on her true passion: art. She was quite an accomplished painter, and she hoped to go on to art school after graduation.

Even though the two girls were identical, their different personalities were clearly reflected in their appearances. Today, for example, Susan wore a tailored white blouse, a navy blue plaid wool skirt, and navy blue knee socks, while her twin sister was decked out in her best pair of jeans and a tomato-red turtleneck sweater. From Chris's ears dangled huge, red-enameled earrings with big, black polka dots. In fact, unless they were actually trying to make the point of their being identical twins, it was difficult to tell that the two girls were even sisters.

Despite their differences, however, the girls got along famously. When they weren't dreaming up clever little schemes—or trying to straighten out the aftermath—they enjoyed spending time together, usually just talking. The two sisters felt they could tell each other everything—and almost always did.

"Look, there's Mr. Peterson!" cried Chris.

By this point, they had reached the attractive white house. And, sure enough, Mr. Peterson was out front, raking leaves. He was a kind man in his sixties who always took time out from his responsibilities at the bookstore to chat with Chris and Susan about their favorite books. He enjoyed talking to the twins, and today was no exception.

"Good morning!" the girls called.

Mr. Peterson looked up from the pile of leaves he was concentrating on and waved.

"Hello, Chris! Hi, Susan!" He gave them both a big smile. "How are my favorite twins this morning?"

"Just fine, Mr. Peterson," Susan replied. "It's nice and early, so we're taking our time walking to school."

"How about you?" asked Chris. "I thought you were usually at the store by now, getting ready to open. Is everything all right?"

Mr. Peterson's smile faded. "Well, not exactly. I'm afraid Mrs. Peterson will be opening the store by herself today. As soon as I get this yard cleaned up, I'm going to go over to Westfield to take a look at that new retirement home that just opened up there."

Susan gasped. "Don't tell me you and Mrs. Peterson are planning to retire!"

"Oh, no, it's not for us. It's for my sister, Cecilia Carpenter."

"Oh, yes, Mrs. Carpenter. I didn't know she was your sister," said Chris. "She lives on Crabtree Hill in that big, old Victorian house, doesn't she?"

Mr. Peterson frowned. "Not for long. No, I'm afraid my sister has gotten it into her head that the house she's been living in for almost thirty years is haunted."

"Haunted!" the twins cried in unison.

"That's right. She claims there have been all kinds of

peculiar things going on there at night lately, and she believes that ghosts are responsible."

"But that's ridiculous!" Susan was indignant. "There's no such thing as ghosts." She remembered only too well the summer before, when it seemed as if ghosts were making mischief at Camp Pinewood . . . and it turned out that it was someone very *real* who was behind it all.

"Well, my wife Ellie and I haven't been very successful at convincing Cecilia of that. Our house is just too small for a third person, so we really don't have any other choice but to look into a retirement home. Besides," he went on thoughtfully, "Ellie and I can't help wondering what it means, the way Cecilia has been imagining all these things. Maybe she'd be better off in a retirement home."

Chris and Susan exchanged glances. They could tell from Mr. Peterson's tone that even though he was worried about his sister, he didn't believe that for one minute.

"Enough about my troubles," Mr. Peterson suddenly said, his voice hearty. "You two had better be on your way. I don't want you to be late for school on my account."

"I guess we'd better." Susan was reluctant to go, however. Mr. Peterson was obviously very upset by his sister's irrational belief that her beautiful Victorian house, with its turrets and towers and gingerbread trim, was haunted. And, as usual, she wished there was some way she could help. "We'll be seeing you soon. I've been meaning to stop in your store to get some new books. Now that it's getting colder, I love curling up in front of the fireplace with some good reading!"

She tried to sound cheerful. It wasn't until she and Chris had continued on their way and Mr. Peterson was out of earshot, that she let on how very concerned she was.

"Isn't that terrible?" she asked her twin. "Imagine, poor Mrs. Carpenter having to go live in a retirement home and give up that huge, gorgeous house on Crabtree Hill. And all because she thinks it's haunted!"

"Well, maybe it *is* haunted."

"Christine Pratt! You know that's impossible!" Susan thought for a second, then added, "Isn't it?"

"I don't know. There are certainly enough documented cases of haunted houses. You know, places where strange things happen, and no one can account for them, no matter how hard they try. Maybe the house on Crabtree Hill is one of those houses!"

Susan remained silent. She refused to believe that her sister was right. Saying that a house might really be haunted wasn't just being playful, at least not in this case. Not if Cecilia Carpenter was ready to move out because of it.

"Well, whether the house is haunted or not, I'm afraid there's not much we can do to help the Petersons and Mrs. Carpenter," Chris went on. "I really wish we could, but it sounds like it's purely a family affair."

"I suppose so." Susan was still troubled, but she knew Chris was right. There really wasn't anything they could do. She decided to put the whole thing out of her mind—at least for now.

"Hey, I've got a great idea," she said suddenly. "Let's go for a long bike ride after school. It's the perfect day for it. We could even head over to the Atkinses' farm and pick up some pumpkins. Think we could manage to balance one or two in our bicycle baskets?"

"I'll bet we could. . . . Oh, wait a minute. I just remembered something. The first meeting of the Halloween Dance Committee is today, right after school. I don't know how long it'll run."

"That's okay," her sister assured her cheerfully. "We've still got weeks and weeks of this fantastic weather ahead of us. We'll have other chances for bike riding."

"How about tomorrow?"

"You're on—just as long as I'm not swamped with homework. If we go, I'll even spring for ice cream cones at Fozzy's on our way home."

"In that case, you can *definitely* count me in!"

"Speaking of the Halloween Dance," said Susan, "how's it coming? I assume good old Whittington High will be holding its usual masquerade party in the school gym. Black and orange crêpe-paper streamers and balloons, all the cider and doughnuts you can eat, bobbing for apples, a prize for the scariest costume . . ."

Chris wrinkled her nose. "Sounds pretty predictable, doesn't it?"

"Not at all! I *love* all those things! It wouldn't seem like Halloween without them!"

"I know." Chris was suddenly pensive. "It's just that I was wondering if we could come up with something different for a change. You know, make the Halloween Dance *special* in some way. That's why I decided to join the dance committee in the first place, as a matter of fact. I'm going to suggest exactly that at the meeting today."

"Do you have any ideas?" asked Susan.

"Nope. Not yet." Chris tugged on one of the red plastic combs that pulled her hair back on either side of her face. "I don't even have any ideas for a costume yet, much less for the dance. But I was hoping that I'd be able to think up *something*."

"You will." With a huge grin, Susan added, "After all, isn't that what we Pratt twins are famous for? Coming up with crazy, off-the-wall ideas?"

"I'll say!" Chris returned. "In face, sometimes we even manage to pull them off!"

"We *always* manage to pull them off! At least we always have in the past."

"Let's just hope we can keep on batting a thousand, then," Chris said with a chuckle. "At any rate, I'm sure I'll be able to come up with an idea sooner or later. Maybe the meeting after school today will inspire me. I do some of my best work under pressure."

By that point, the two girls had reached the schoolyard. Streams of students were making their way toward the stately red-brick building. As they joined the others who were heading for the main entrance, Chris suddenly snapped her fingers.

"I just remembered that I have to stop off at my locker before homeroom. I have a math quiz first period, and I want to look over my notes before then."

Susan just smiled. She was only too aware that math was her sister's very best subject and that she would undoubtedly manage a perfect score on the quiz even without any last-minute studying.

"Okay. See you later, then."

"Hey, do me a favor, Sooz. See if you can think of any new ideas for the Halloween Dance, okay? Doughnuts and orange balloons may be fun, but I'm determined to come up with something unusual this year. I really meant it when I said I wanted to make this one dance that we'll never forget!"

Little did Chris suspect, as she hurried off to the side entrance of the school that was closest to her locker, that it would, indeed, prove to be exactly that: a Halloween Dance that neither she nor her twin would ever forget.

Two

Even though it was still early, the halls of Whittington High were already crowded with students. Some were strolling over to their homerooms, obviously reluctant to begin another day of school on such a beautiful morning. Others stood in front of their lockers, sorting through textbooks and notebooks and sports equipment in an effort to get ready for a full day of classes. And still others were using the few minutes before the final warning bell to chat with their friends.

It was, in fact, the ideal time for stopping to have a quick conversation with someone one didn't ordinarily run into during the course of the normal school day. Katy Johnson was such a person. As Chris wove through the throngs of students, she spotted Katy talking to two of her girlfriends. Math notes were momentarily forgotten as she made a beeline for an old friend she saw only too rarely.

"Katy! Katy!" Chris called, edging over to the group.

The redheaded girl glanced up. As soon as she realized that it was Christine Pratt who was calling her name, her face lit up. After all, the two girls had known each other since kindergarten, when they had met discovering a shared passion for building the tallest towers possible out of colored wooden blocks.

"Well, if it isn't Chris Pratt! I haven't seen you in *ages*! How are you? Where have you been hiding yourself lately?"

Chris laughed. "I'm fine, Katy. And I've been busy with the usual things. You know me . . . always twenty-five hours worth of things to get done in every twenty-four-hour period. How about you?"

"Keeping busy, too. I'm on the school's gymnastic team this year, and—"

"As if I didn't know! As if all of Whittington High didn't know! Why, you're the best thing that's ever happened to girls' sports in this town! School's only been in session for a few weeks, and already you've managed to win—what is it—*two* meets?"

"Well . . ." Katy blushed, embarrassed by Christine's praise. But it was obvious that she was pleased as well. "At any rate, I've been pretty busy with that. We have gymnastics practice almost every day after school. Ms. Barlow works us all pretty hard!"

"Well, it's certainly paying off. I heard that your routine on the uneven parallel bars has been totally astounding every judge who's seen it!"

Chris's praise of Katy Johnson's athletic abilities was well-founded. Although she was just over five feet tall and weighed in at barely one hundred pounds, Katy was a natural athlete. Combined with her strength was a certain grace that invariably gave her performance that special

12

something the judges always looked for, whether she was on the parallel bars, the horse, the balance beam, or the mats doing free-style exercises.

And with her freckles, bright green eyes, and curly red hair, which was usually worn down around her shoulders, as it was today, but was pulled back in a ponytail during competitions, she made many people think of a little elf as she expertly ran through her well-practiced routines. Katy Johnson was, without a doubt, Whittington High's best female athlete.

"By the way," Katy said, "do you know Carolyn and Jennifer?"

Chris hadn't met Katy's two friends before, and the four girls chatted amiably for a minute or two.

"Well, Katy, I've really got to get going," Jennifer said. "My homeroom's all the way on the other side of the school, over by the science labs. As it is, I'm going to have to make a run for it."

"I've got to go, too," Carolyn agreed. "Nice meeting you, Chris. See you around, Katy!"

Chris was glad that she and Katy had a moment to talk by themselves.

"I really wish we could get together sometime soon," said Chris. "I know Susan would love to see you, too. In fact, we were just talking about going for a long bike ride one of these days. This autumn weather is perfect for that kind of thing. Maybe you could join us after gymnastics practice some afternoon."

"Maybe. I'd really like that. If I'm not too wiped out, that is," she added with a rueful grin.

"Great. We thought we might head over to the Atkinses' farm to pick up some pumpkins. . . ."

"Pumpkins! Is it Halloween *already*?"

Chris laughed. "I guess Ms. Barlow really has been keeping you busy! Sure, Halloween is just three weeks away now."

"Believe it or not, I've been so wrapped up in getting ready for our next meet that I haven't given it a single thought!"

"Well, you'd better start thinking about a costume," Chris teased. "You don't want to be the only one at the Halloween Dance without one!"

Instead of looking pleased at the reminder that one of Whittington High's most popular events was only a few weeks away, Katy's expression darkened.

"Getting a costume together is the last thing I have to be concerned about," she said seriously.

Chris was surprised. "Why, Katy! Aren't you planning to come? I'm sure it'll be lots of fun! In fact, I joined the Halloween Dance Committee to help make *sure* it'll be lots of fun!"

Katy just shook her head slowly. "I don't know, Chris. I'm not very good at going to that kind of thing alone. I always feel silly standing around and waiting for somebody to ask me to dance. And I feel even sillier if no one *does*!"

"What if someone invited you? Would you go if you had a date?"

"Well, sure! But I really don't think that's going to happen."

"Why not?" Chris was genuinely puzzled.

Katy, however, was ready with an explanation. "Oh, Chris, I'm not like you! I don't have half a dozen boys dying to take me out, calling me every night and begging for a date! I'm not the president of this and the chairperson for that, the way you are. I'm simply not one of the most popular girls around school."

"But that doesn't mean no one will ask you to the dance, Katy! You don't have to be on a million committees just to get a date!"

"I know," Katy sighed. "But, frankly, Chris, I don't know too many boys. I'm basically very shy. I'm not good at talking to them. And, besides, girls' gymnastics takes up so much of my time that I don't even have that many opportunities to *meet* any boys."

Chris felt bad for her friend. She seemed so resigned to the fact that she couldn't get a date for the Halloween Dance and so determined not to go alone or even with some of her girlfriends. But Chris refused to let it pass.

"Well, if someone *were* going to ask you to the dance, who would you want it to be?"

"Oh, I don't know, Chris. . . ."

"Come on, Katy! You can be honest with me. I won't tell, I promise. There must be *somebody* around school that you've got your eye on."

"Well, there is one boy . . ."

"Who?"

Katy glanced around furtively, as if the last thing she wanted was for anyone to overhear. "Do you know Wayne Lowell?"

"Of course I do! He's in my English class, as a matter of fact. I see him every day."

"To tell you the truth, I wouldn't mind going to the Halloween Dance with him. I think he's one of the sweetest boys I've ever met."

"He *is* awfully nice," Chris agreed.

Inwardly, however, she groaned. It was true that Wayne Lowell was nice, but he was undoubtedly one of the *shyest* boys in their class as well. The chances of him mustering up the courage to ask Katy, or anyone else, to the Halloween

Dance were about as remote as . . . as Chris turning into a bat and flying through the corridors of Whittington High.

"At any rate," Katy said a bit sadly, "there's no point in worrying about it. I'm sure I'll have a perfectly wonderful time on Halloween helping my mother hand out candy to the trick-or-treaters. I just love seeing all the kids in the neighborhood dressed up in their cute little costumes."

"Sure. That sounds like a lot of fun."

Just then, the last warning bell sounded. Chris and Katy both grimaced.

"We'd better get going," said Chris, "or we'll be late for homeroom. I still have to stop off at my locker." She wrinkled her nose. "Math quiz today, first period."

"Well, good luck, Chris. Not that you'll need it. And, listen, let's try to go on that bike ride really soon, okay?"

"Great. I'll call you, Katy!"

As Chris dashed off to her locker in pursuit of her math notebook, it was not the factoring of algebraic equations that she was thinking about. It was Katy Johnson—and her dilemma. She had so much going for her, yet because she was too busy to meet many boys—and too shy to talk to those she *did* meet—she had to miss out on something like the Halloween Dance. If only there were some way she could help . . .

But maybe there was.

After all, Chris was not one to let the chance to play matchmaker slip by. Already her mind was clicking away. Maybe, just maybe, part of her unusual idea for this year's dance would include a way that *everybody* could participate—whether or not he or she had a date—without letting shyness or anything else get in the way. She was more determined than ever to wrack her brain until she came up with some solution. There was absolutely no reason in the world why someone like Katy Johnson should have to miss out on something that was as much fun as a costume party!

Goodness! It's been quite a day, thought Chris as she slammed the door of her locker. First such bad news about Mr. Peterson's sister, on the verge of giving up her home because she believes it's haunted. And now, problems with Katy's social life . . .

But there was no time for worrying about either right now. Chris tried to force herself to start thinking about her math quiz as she ran off to her homeroom. After all, she reminded herself, first things first.

But the very moment that's over, she vowed, I'm going to become totally single-minded. Maybe I can't help Cecilia Carpenter, but I'm going to find a way to get Katy and Wayne Lowell together, or at least get Katy to that dance!

And once she set her mind to something, Chris knew, she always—*always*—saw it through.

Three

For the rest of the day, Chris found it difficult to concentrate on any of her schoolwork. Even during the math quiz, visions of those orange and black streamers and balloons that Susan had mentioned kept dancing before her eyes— even as she was trying to solve the longest algebraic equation she had ever seen.

Of course there are some things that simply *have* to be a part of every Halloween celebration, she kept thinking. But, somehow, there just *has* to be more!

By the time the last bell of the day rang, right after her eighth-period French class, Chris couldn't wait to get to the meeting of the dance committee. Maybe one of the other members would have come up with a super idea . . .

The turnout for the meeting was better than Chris had expected. Betsy Carter, this year's chairperson, also seemed surprised. As she called the meeting to order right on time, she looked around the biology lab, the classroom in which this first meeting was being held. There were half a dozen students there besides Chris and Betsy.

Chris recognized all of them, from classes or other club meetings, except for one. A boy with sandy blond hair sat in the back, slightly apart from all the others. He was good-looking, and she noticed him with surprise.

I thought I already knew all the cute boys at school, she thought with amusement. I'd better not let Susan know I missed out on this one. She'll think I'm losing my touch!

The boy was quickly forgotten, however, as the meeting came to order. Chris immediately turned her attention toward Betsy.

"Good afternoon, and welcome!" Betsy began with a smile. "I can already tell that there's a lot of interest in making this year's Halloween Dance a really memorable event. I don't think I've seen so many people at a committee meeting since last year's first Bake Sale meeting, when we made sure everybody knew we'd be sampling brownies made by the home economics classes!"

Everyone laughed, relieved that being on this committee was going to be *fun* besides a lot of hard work.

"Unfortunately, I can't reward you all with brownies this time around," the energetic, dark-haired girl continued. "But I *can* promise you that if we all put our heads together and do some creative thinking, we can come up with a really terrific dance.

"Now, I'd like to get started by listing all of the different things we have to make plans for. Music, of course, and refreshments . . ."

"How about a theme?" suggested Don Ellis, a lanky junior who was known around school for his active participation in the debating club.

"What do you mean?" Connie McCormick asked. She

19

was a soft-spoken senior who didn't join committees very often. "Isn't this going to be a masquerade party? I thought *that* was the theme."

Most of the others murmured in agreement. It was then that Chris raised her hand.

"Yes, Chris?"

"I think I know what Don means. About having a theme, that is."

"You don't like the idea of a costume party?" Betsy sounded surprised.

"Oh, I definitely think everyone should dress up. After all, that's what Halloween is all about, isn't it?" Her sister Susan's words earlier that day popped into her mind. "I think we should keep *all* the Halloween traditions. Wearing costumes, bobbing for apples, decorating the gym in orange and black . . .

"But I'm wondering if we could take the whole thing one step further."

"Sorry, Chris," Betsy said, shaking her head slowly. "I'm afraid I still don't follow."

"Me, either, Chris," Wendy Pierce called out, her tone teasing. "Unless you're talking about one of those practical jokes you Pratt twins are so famous for!"

Chris could feel her cheeks turning pink, but she laughed. It was no secret that she and Susan had always enjoyed both aspects of the "trick or treat" theme.

"Well, to be perfectly honest, I'm not sure what I'm talking about, either. I mean, I know that I'd like to do something different this year. Something that's never been done at Whittington High before. Something that's . . . well, *special*. The only problem is, I don't have any good ideas."

Chris glanced around the room, wearing a sheepish

expression. "I thought maybe somebody here could help me come up with something."

"That's the kind of thing I was thinking about, too," Don Ellis said, this time sounding a bit more sure of himself. "How about having a theme for everyone's costume? Something like the American Revolution. And everybody would have to wear clothes from that period."

"Oh, I *love* that idea!" cried Connie. "The boys could dress up like rebels and redcoats, and the girls could wear those fancy gowns."

"Or how about having 'the future' as our theme?" someone else called out. "We could all come as space travelers!"

"Or creatures from other planets!"

"How about a dance where everybody comes dressed as who—or what—they *wish* they were?" asked Connie. Almost to herself, she added, "I could come dressed as a rock star."

"It seems as if everybody agrees that it's a good idea to have a theme," Betsy said.

She turned to the blackboard and wrote: "Masquerade party with a theme." She underlined the word *theme*. "I guess we should decide on what we want, and then take a vote."

For the next half hour, the group brought up new ideas for themes and then heatedly debated each one. Circus performers, animals, famous historical figures, movie stars— everyone seemed to have a different thought on the matter. And one idea led to another, until Betsy had listed over twenty different possibilities on the blackboard.

By then it was getting late. Don suddenly glanced at the clock and said, "Hey, look what time it is! I've got to get going."

"Me, too," agreed Wendy. "But we still haven't come to any decision."

"I'll tell you what," Betsy said, holding up her hands for silence. "We've all got a lot to think about here. We've got some great ideas, and picking out just one isn't going to be easy. So how about holding off on our final vote until our next meeting? That way, everybody will have a chance to think about it some more. Maybe we can all talk to some of our friends, too, to see which ideas are the most popular."

Everyone agreed that that was a wise thing to do.

"Besides," Don added with a chuckle, "this way we'll all have a chance to come up with even *more* ideas!"

"No, please!" Betsy wailed, laughing. "We already have enough! Let's all put our creativity on hold for a while, okay? All right, I'll see you all next week. In the meantime, see if you can settle on just one of these ideas. Then we can start planning all the details. Decorations, refreshments, music . . . we still have a lot of work to do, everybody!"

As the meeting started to break up, the members of the dance committee chattered away excitedly. They wandered off in twos and threes, debating the pros and cons of each idea for the Halloween Dance theme.

Chris, it appeared, was the only one who had reservations.

It wasn't that she didn't like the idea of having a theme. On the contrary, she thought it was fresh and original. It would, she hoped, inspire the students of Whittington High to come up with some interesting interpretations, some unusual twists in putting together their costumes.

What was troubling her was her conversation earlier that day with Katy Johnson.

Chris had vowed, then and there, to work really hard to make the Halloween Dance one that everybody could participate in. And while the theme idea was a good one, it didn't really make this dance any different from all the others held at Whittington High. Katy wouldn't come to a theme masquerade any more readily than she would come to any other high school dance.

As she wandered out of the classroom, carrying her books and her shoulder bag, Chris was lost in a dream world. In fact, she was so absorbed in her thoughts that she didn't even notice that someone was walking alongside her. That is, not until he spoke to her.

"Excuse me. You're Chris, aren't you?"

She turned to see that the boy with the sandy blond hair had joined her.

"Yes, I am." She was genuinely surprised. "Do you *know* me?"

"Not yet!" he replied with a laugh. "But during the meeting, Betsy called you by name. And, well . . . let's just say I made a point of remembering it."

Chris, usually at ease with boys, could feel her cheeks turning pink. How direct this boy was! Yet she was flattered. More than that; she was pleased. So he had noticed her—just the way she'd noticed him.

"I'm afraid I didn't catch your name," she said as they strolled out of the biology lab together.

"It's . . . My friends call me B.J."

"B.J.! That's original!"

"B.J. Wilkins. I suppose we should introduce ourselves formally." He grinned and extended his hand.

Chris was already beginning to feel much more relaxed with this boy. Perhaps he was a bit more honest than most boys she knew, but she was also beginning to find him quite charming.

"I'm Christine Pratt." She smiled and shook his hand. "Are you a senior here at Whittington?"

"Yup. And I know exactly what your next question is going to be."

"Are you a mind reader?"

"I could pretend that I am, I suppose, but then you'd probably want me to tell you what you're going to be when you grow up and what presents you're going to get for Christmas and all kinds of things like that, and I'd be found out. No, I'm not a mind reader at all. To be perfectly honest, I've already had this conversation with different people about a million times."

"Oh, really? So what *is* my next question, then?" Chris asked impishly.

In a high voice, B.J. said, " 'Then how come I've never seen you before?' "

Chris laughed at his teasing imitation. "You're right! That *is* what I was going to ask you next! And what's the answer?"

In his normal voice, he said, "Because my family just moved here a couple of weeks ago. We didn't even make it to Whittington in time for the start of school. So," he added with a shrug, "I guess I'm what you'd call the new kid on the block."

"In that case, welcome to Whittington!" Chris looked at this curious "new" boy a bit more closely. She liked his friendliness and his sense of humor. He was the type of boy that one didn't forget easily. And his blue eyes and wide grin weren't easy to ignore, either.

"I thank you from the bottom of my heart." He bowed dramatically, meanwhile making a sweeping gesture with his right arm. "But it wasn't *me* I wanted to talk to you about. It was what you said in the meeting just now. About having a special twist to this Halloween Dance—my very first social event at Whittington High, I might add."

"Is that why you joined the committee?" Chris asked jokingly. "To make sure you wouldn't be disappointed?"

"Would you believe I joined because I'd heard rumors that Christine Pratt was also on the committee? No, huh? Well, then, would you believe I joined because I thought it might be a good way to get to know some of the kids here? I don't want to be the new kid forever, you know!"

"That makes sense. And it's working, too. You've already met me!"

"That's right. See, it's already proven worth the effort. But to get back to your idea, I think it was a good one."

"Thanks. Unfortunately, we sort of got off the subject. I mean, I *like* the idea of having a theme for everyone's costume, but . . ."

"But what?"

Chris sighed. "Well, to make a long story short, I was hoping the committee would be able to come up with an idea that would let *all* of the students come to the dance, whether they had dates or not."

B.J. looked puzzled. "Is that some kind of rule at Whittington High? You're not allowed to go to a school dance unless you've got a date?"

"Oh, no! But some of the girls—and the boys, too, I imagine—are too shy to go alone or even with their friends." Katy Johnson's exact words were still fresh in her mind. "They say they feel silly standing around, waiting for somebody to ask them to dance."

"Yeah, I see what you mean. I know I wouldn't like to go to the dance alone. Especially since I hardly know anybody."

"Believe it or not, some of the kids who've gone to

school here for years don't know a lot of the others, either. They're too shy or too busy with other things. At any rate, I thought that since I was on the committee and all, I might be able to come up with something to change all that. That's why I brought it up in the first place. But, well, we all got off the track somehow." There was disappointment in Chris's tone as she finished her little speech.

"It was a noble thought," B.J. said, sounding sympathetic. "But it's not too late. Since we didn't actually decide on one particular theme, I don't think anybody would be too upset if we came up with something entirely different."

"Well, I intend to think about it all week. In fact, I think I'll get my sister involved, too. She comes up with the best ideas."

"Really? Then I won't give it a second thought. If there are *two* Pratt girls working on the Halloween Dance, I've got nothing to worry about!"

By then, Chris and B.J. had reached the school's front entrance, where the main corridor divided into two narrower hallways.

"I've got to stop at my locker," said Chris. "It's down this way."

"Since I have to go this way, I guess we'll have to part." B.J. snapped his fingers. "And here I'd been thinking that this was my lucky day. Oh, well. But at least I know I'll be seeing you again soon."

"Right. At the next dance committee meeting."

"Or," he said with a mischievous gleam in his blue eyes, "maybe even sooner. Who knows? All kinds of mysterious things have been known to happen around Halloween."

"That's funny." Chris laughed. "I was saying the exact same thing just this morning."

"Aha! So maybe I really *am* a mind reader, and I just

never realized it before! All right, Christine Pratt, I'll say good-bye now. But at the risk of sounding like an incurable romantic, let me add that I'm already counting the minutes until our next rendezvous!"

As Chris turned down the hall, after waving good-bye to B.J. one last time, she was having the exact same thought. That, and one other: She couldn't *wait* to tell Susan all about B.J. Wilkins!

Four

Susan closed the thick library book she'd just been reading with a loud, thoughtful sigh. What a wonderful, romantic story *Gone With the Wind* was! She'd already read it twice, yet when she'd spotted it on the shelf, she couldn't resist taking it down and leafing through it one more time, finding her favorite sections and rereading them.

How easily she'd slipped back in time, into the world of that feisty heroine, Scarlett O'Hara! The long, narrow tables and high bookshelves of the Whittington High School library had vanished, and in their place was the Old South, filled with Yankees and Rebels and beautiful girls in luscious silk ball gowns.

I'd love to wear a dress like that, Susan thought wistfully as she returned the book to the shelf where she'd found it. Just once, for just one night . . .

Maybe for Halloween! Yes, a Scarlett O'Hara–type dress, one with puffed sleeves and a ruffle around the neck-

28

line and a full, floor-length skirt . . . And it would have to be one of her favorite colors: a peachy pink, a pale turquoise blue, or perhaps lemon yellow . . .

It was the perfect idea for a costume. Susan decided that, as soon as she got home, she'd ask her mother to help her make a dress like that. With the Halloween Dance still three whole weeks away, there should be plenty of time.

She glanced at the clock above the main entrance of the school library and discovered that it was much later than she'd thought. Here she was supposed to be researching a science paper on the human heart, and instead she'd been lost in the world of Scarlett O'Hara and Rhett Butler. She knew she had to get going. Not only had she promised to start dinner for her family, but the school library was about to close.

As she strolled down First Street a few minutes later, she was still caught up in the romance of the book she'd been reading. If only she were as spunky as the heroine of that wonderful novel! And if only she could meet someone as dashing and romantic as Captain Rhett Butler . . .

She was so wrapped up in her little dreamworld that she stepped off the curb and into the street without looking.

"Watch out!" someone suddenly yelled, in a voice that was nearly hysterical.

Susan turned and saw a boy on a bicycle careening toward her at top speed. Just in time she stepped backward, up onto the curb. A split second later and he might have crashed into her.

Shaken, she just stood there, unable to move. The boy immediately screeched to a halt and jumped off his bike.

"Are you all right?" he asked anxiously, hurrying over to her side.

"I-I guess I am." Susan blinked. "What exactly happened?"

"I'm not sure. All I know is that I was making a right turn off First Street, and the next thing I knew, there you were, right in front of me. One thing I *am* sure of, though. I had a green light."

"Oh, dear. It was all my fault, then. I should have looked before I started to cross. I was daydreaming, I'm afraid."

"Gee, I guess it was partly my fault, too." The boy was suddenly apologetic. "I was going a little fast." Sheepishly he added, "I was in a hurry to get home. It's kind of late, and . . ."

"Well, what really matters is that neither of us was hurt."

"Are you sure about that? You look a little pale."

"You do, too."

Susan studied the boy more closely. He had sandy blond hair, blue eyes, and good-looking features. He looked as if he were about her age, yet she was almost certain that she had never seen him before. "Do you go to Whittington High?"

He broke into a wide smile. "Don't worry. I'm willing to give you my name and address in case you decide you want to turn me in to the Reckless Bicycle-Rider Patrol."

Susan laughed. Suddenly, the whole episode didn't seem like such a catastrophe after all.

"I'm not planning to turn you in to anybody. I was just curious, since I don't think I've ever seen you around here before."

"That's very possible. My family and I just moved here a few weeks ago. I'm B.J. Wilkins."

"Pleased to meet you, B.J. My name is Susan Pratt. Do you go to Whittington High?"

"I sure do. I'm a senior there."

"Me, too!"

"Well, then," he teased, "you and I have a lot more in common than having come this close to having an accident."

"I really am sorry about that. I should be more careful. It's just that I was thinking about this book I was reading . . ."

"Don't apologize. Let's just agree that we were both at fault. Fifty-fifty. Okay?"

"It's a deal!"

Susan and B.J. stood awkwardly for a few seconds. Neither knew how to continue their conversation—and Susan, for one, certainly didn't want it to end so soon.

"Where did your family move here from?" she finally asked.

"From a tiny town called Pottersville. Ever hear of it?"

She thought for a moment, then shook her head. "No, I don't think so."

"I'm not surprised." B.J. laughed. "It's only about thirty miles from here, but it's so small that I don't think they even bother to put it on those road maps they have at gas stations."

Susan was still afraid that once she and B.J. went off on their separate ways, she would never run into him again—either on *or* off his bicycle. Her mind was clicking away.

What would Chris do if she were in my place? she wondered. She's so much better at meeting boys than I am. If she had just met someone like B.J., somebody she really liked, what would *she* do?

The answer came to her almost instantly.

Of course, she thought. Chris would offer to show him around town, since he's new here and all. And she'd probably suggest that they stop off at Fozzy's for an ice cream cone!

But Susan wasn't as brave as Chris. That kind of thing didn't come quite as easily to her as it did to her twin sister. She stood in front of B.J., clutching her schoolbooks to her chest, agonizing over exactly how to phrase her invitation.

And so she was totally astonished when he said, "Listen, Susan, if you're not in a hurry, how about stopping off at that ice cream parlor down the street? What's it called? Fozzy's? I hear they stuff as much ice cream as is humanly possible into a cone."

Susan's mouth dropped open. "You must be a mind reader!"

B.J. grinned. "That's funny; people are always saying that about me! So how about it, Susan?"

"But I thought you were in a hurry!"

"Well, maybe getting home can wait a *little* longer . . ."

A few minutes later, Susan and B.J. were strolling down First Street, armed with two of the biggest chocolate-chip ice cream cones either of them had ever seen. It was difficult for B.J. to walk his bicycle and eat at the same time, but his efforts at doing just that provided both of them with almost constant bursts of hysterical laughter. When they weren't making jokes about the difficulties of living on a planet where there was gravity, Susan was pointing out some of Whittington's more notable landmarks.

"Down that street is Whittington's town park. We've got a brand-new monument there, commemorating the town's founders. In fact, Whittington just celebrated its one-hundredth anniversary this past summer."

"No kidding! Hey, what about that house up there on that hill? Looks kind of spooky, if you ask me!"

Susan glanced up toward Crabtree Hill, where the huge Victorian house that belonged to Cecilia Carpenter loomed, looking as if it could, indeed, be haunted.

"I guess it does look sort of spooky," she agreed. "But as far as I know, it's not."

Even as she said those words, however, she felt uneasy. Maybe it really *was* haunted. Or perhaps there was *something* going on there—other than an old woman's overactive imagination—that was scaring Mrs. Carpenter away. While she had tried to put this morning's conversation with Mr. Peterson out of her mind, she couldn't help wondering what was really going on. If only she could find out more about the "ghosts" that were troubling Mrs. Carpenter!

But Susan remembered her sister's contention that the whole thing was "a family affair." As much as she wanted to get involved, she couldn't really see any way to do that. At least not at this point. Instead, she decided to concentrate on B.J.

"That house belongs to one of Whittington's longtime residents, a woman named Cecilia Carpenter. She's the sister of the people who live over here—the Petersons. They run the bookstore in town. You know, that little shop that's right next door to Fozzy's."

Those three fat pumpkins that Susan and Chris had spotted early that same day were still sitting on the Petersons' porch, bright splashes of orange against the whiteness of the boxy house. But something was different now.

All three of them had had faces carved into them. And all three of them were wearing huge, mischievous grins.

"Oooh, look at the jack-o'-lanterns!" Susan squealed.

"I guess Halloween is just around the corner."

"Yes, it's only a few weeks away now."

She was tempted to tell B.J. about her twin sister's whimsical theory, the Pumpkin Principle. But it sounded so silly now. Although Chris had just been joking, it would be difficult to explain. Imagine, pretending that pumpkins had some mysterious power over people, the power to make them want to play tricks and pretend to be someone they weren't! Even though thinking about it made her chuckle, she decided not to say anything to B.J. about it.

Instead, she said, "You know, Whittington High sponsors a Halloween Dance every year. It's a big costume party, and it's always lots of fun." She hesitated, then added, "You might want to go to it. After all, it would be a good way to meet some of the kids in the senior class. Since you're new in town and all."

B.J. looked at her and smiled. "I don't think I'm doing too badly. I mean, in terms of meeting people here. In fact, I seem to have a knack for, shall we say, *running into* some of the nicer ones!"

Susan could feel herself blushing. He certainly didn't waste any time making his feelings known! Yet she was pleased. She liked this new boy. As a matter of fact, she liked him *a lot*.

Who knows? she thought. Maybe B.J. and I will go to the Halloween Dance *together*.

Instantly, an image of herself dressed in one of those fancy Scarlett O'Hara–style dresses popped into her mind.

And, almost as quickly, she pictured B.J. standing beside her, wearing the type of outfit that Captain Rhett Butler himself might have worn.

By now, Susan was *really* blushing. She kept her eyes on the last of her chocolate-chip ice cream, pretending to be totally absorbed in licking all of the ice cream out of the bottom of the cone. She was relieved when B.J. suddenly changed the subject.

"Well, Susan, I live over that way, on Cherry Street." He pointed down one of the roads that branched off First Street.

"Oh, really? I live over *that* way." She pointed in the opposite direction.

"No kidding." B.J. paused for a minute, as if he were trying to decide whether or not to say what was on his mind. "Hey, I have an idea," he finally said.

Susan could tell that he was trying to make his "idea" sound casual, and she listened with interest.

"How about if I walk you home? That way, I'd get to see a part of Whittington I've never seen before. Of course, this is all in the interest of getting to know my brand-new hometown." His playful grin, however, indicated that he had no desire to hide his true reasons for offering to walk her home.

Smiling to herself, Susan nodded. This B.J. Wilkins was certainly one of the most direct boys she had ever met!

"Okay. To give you the chance to see a new neighborhood, of course."

B.J. just grinned.

As they walked toward the Pratts' home, Susan found herself telling him all about her interest in art. She was taking two art classes at school this year, she explained, one in drawing still lifes—things like bowls of fruit and vases of flowers—and one in painting. And in her spare time, she was trying to do as many finished drawings and paintings as she could.

"You see, I want to go to art school next year, after graduation," she said to B.J. "When I apply, I have to show them my best work. So I'm trying really hard to do some nice pieces."

"Maybe you'll show them to me one of these days," B.J. suggested. "That is, if you're not shy about showing people what you've done."

It was true that Susan was shy about a lot of things, but displaying her artwork did not happen to be one of them.

"I'd *love* to show you some of my paintings! I've got dozens. Maybe even hundreds!"

"Great!"

They had reached the Pratts' house by then.

"Well, this is where I live," said Susan, gesturing toward the gray house with the blue shingles.

"So I guess this is the end of the tour."

"Unless you'd like to come in for a while . . ."

"Thanks, but I've really got to get home. Boy, they really pile on the homework at Whittington High, don't they? Just for tonight, I've got enough to keep me busy for an entire weekend!"

B.J. hopped onto his bicycle. "Well, Susan, I'm really glad me met. I just wish our introduction had been a little bit . . . calmer."

"I'm sure I'll be seeing you around school," said Susan. "You bet!"

With that, B.J. broke into his wide grin and was off.

Susan stood on the front lawn for a few seconds, watching him pedal away. Meeting a boy on her way home from school today was the *last* thing she'd expected. Especially one who was as much fun as B.J.!

As she went into the house, just the slightest bit reluctantly, one thought was clear in Susan's mind.

She couldn't *wait* to tell Chris all about B.J. Wilkins!

Five

When she stopped off at her locker, Chris was still keyed up over the encounter she'd just had with the new boy. But it wasn't long before she was snapped back to reality. As she gathered the books she would need for the evening's homework assignments, she remembered that she needed a pocket dictionary for English class. And thinking about that reminded her that she also needed shampoo, a new notebook for math, and some hand lotion. . . .

Oh, well, I guess it's time for a little shopping spree, she thought. Telling Susan all about the newest development in my social life will simply have to wait.

But as Chris stopped at a few of Whittington's stores, she was in wonderful spirits. Everything she did seemed just a little bit more fun, given her lighthearted mood. She kept thinking about B.J. Wilkins. How much she'd enjoyed talking to him . . . and how much she was looking forward to seeing him again. Even her dismay over the

37

meeting of the dance committee and her inability to communicate successfully her desire to open up the dance to everyone, slipped to the back of her mind.

Everything seemed perfect. That is, until she stopped into Petersons' Bookstore and saw the long face of Mr. Peterson.

"Hello, Chris. What can I do for you today?"

"I need a pocket dictionary, Mr. Peterson. Is anything wrong?"

The white-haired man didn't even smile as he pulled three different pocket dictionaries off a shelf behind the counter and placed them before Chris so that she could choose one. "It's my sister. I took her to see that retirement home this morning. Oh, it was nice enough. It's just that I can't help thinking that Cecilia doesn't really *belong* in a place like that. Why, she's perfectly happy being on her own, taking care of herself, living in that beautiful house of hers. . . .

"But she keeps on insisting that it's not a safe place for anyone to live. She's convinced that there are ghosts there. I know the whole thing sounds ridiculous . . ."

"Maybe she's not just imagining things, Mr. Peterson. Maybe she really has been hearing things, or seeing things, or whatever it is she claims has been going on."

"I suppose that's possible. But by now, I've tried everything. Talking to her, reasoning with her—even suggesting that Ellie and I move in with her. But she says she's afraid for all of us. No, she's determined to get out as soon as she can."

"That's too bad. Gee, Mr. Peterson, I wish there was something I could do to help."

"Thanks, Chris." His smile showed how much he appreciated her concern. "But this really isn't your problem. Now, which dictionary suits your needs best?"

Chris pretended to be intent on examining the three different volumes. But she was still thinking about Mrs. Carpenter's insistence that her house was haunted. And wondering what, if anything, she and Susan could do to help. It was obvious that Mr. Peterson felt the whole thing was hopeless and wouldn't be open to any suggestions. If only she and Sooz could come up with something on their own . . .

She decided to talk to her twin about it, the very first chance she got.

It was late by the time Chris reached the street on which the Pratts lived. She hurried toward the house, anxious to find her sister. She wanted to discuss Cecilia Carpenter's "ghosts" with Susan, but, even more than that, she couldn't wait to tell her all about B.J. Wilkins. In fact, she felt as if she were about to burst at any minute.

And then she stopped, suddenly frozen to the spot.

There in front of her, a few hundred feet ahead, was her twin sister, walking with someone, talking and laughing and acting as if she were having the time of her life.

And the person she was walking with was none other than B.J. Wilkins.

Chris's immediate reaction was to hide. Quickly, she stepped behind the trunk of a huge oak tree. She knew she was being silly, but she wanted to get a better look, to make sure she really was seeing what she *thought* she was seeing.

Sure enough, it was Susan and B.J.

There was no mistaking them. Her own twin, of course, she could recognize a mile away. And the boy with her was certainly B.J. Even though she couldn't see his face all that clearly, he was dressed in dark pants and a Whittington High jacket—just as B.J. had been when she left him less than an hour earlier.

Chris was totally confused. And terribly hurt.

39

You need some time to think, she told herself. Before you jump to any conclusions, take a few deep breaths, go for a walk around the block. If nothing else, the fresh air will do you good.

A few minutes later, Chris headed into the house. She'd thought about the situation and decided that the best thing to do was to reserve judgment until she found out more about it. Walking around the neighborhood wasn't going to help her accomplish anything. And, besides, her schoolbooks were getting heavy.

As Chris let herself into the house, she heard someone rattling pots and pans in the kitchen. She remembered that it was Susan's turn to start dinner tonight, and she rushed to the back of the house in search of her twin.

Sure enough, Susan was in the kitchen with a bright flowered apron tied over her navy blue plaid skirt and crisp white blouse. She was running cold water from the faucet into a saucepan, obviously about to cook the head of broccoli that had been cut into flowerets and was now waiting on the wooden cutting board beside the sink.

As soon as Susan spotted her sister, however, her dinner preparations were forgotten.

"Oh, Chris! You'll *never* guess what happened to me just now on my way home from school!"

"What?"

"I'll tell you all the details in a minute, but I won't keep you in suspense in the meantime. Chris, I met the most terrific boy in the whole wide world! He's nice, and he's cute, and he has the most wonderful smile! His family just moved to Whittington—and his name is B.J. Wilkins!"

Chris gulped—and then forced herself to smile. "Oh, really? And how—how did you meet this—this . . ."

"B.J. B.J. Wilkins. Isn't that a great name? Anyway, it

was the funniest thing. Well, maybe not *funny* exactly . . ."

Susan was waving a wooden spoon as she spoke. Her eyes were bright, her cheeks flushed a bright pink. Chris couldn't remember the last time she'd seen her twin sister so excited. And it was all because of this new boy, this B.J. Wilkins. . . .

"It happened while I was walking home from school. I'd stayed late to do some research at the library. I mean, I was *supposed* to be doing research, but I ended up rereading my favorite parts of *Gone With the Wind* instead. Anyway, as I was on my way home, I was daydreaming about Rhett Butler instead of watching where I was going, and the next thing I knew . . ."

Susan proceeded to tell Chris all about her close call with B.J. and his bicycle and the happy ending to the near accident. She went on to describe him in detail: his sandy blond hair, his blue eyes, his impish grin—and, most of all, his directness and his sense of humor.

". . . and he said he wants to see my artwork sometime. Isn't that wonderful, Chris? I can already tell that he's someone special. Not your ordinary, run-of-the-mill high school boy. Not at all!"

"Gee, that's really great." Chris tried to sound enthusiastic for her sister's sake. But even though she was usually pretty good at acting, this time she just couldn't manage to sound convincing.

Her peculiar reaction did not escape her twin.

"What's the matter, Chris?" Susan was suddenly concerned. She sat down at the kitchen table and began toying with the pepper shaker. "You don't seem very happy for me. Is there anything wrong?"

"Wrong? Oh, no. What makes you think there's anything wrong, Sooz?"

Susan frowned. "You just look a bit . . . I don't know, *distracted*. As if you're a million miles away."

Chris did some fast thinking. "I guess I'm just worried about Mrs. Carpenter. I stopped by the bookstore on my way home from school today, and Mr. Peterson is so upset. He took his sister to look at that retirement home this morning. And she's ready to get rid of her house and move into that home all because she believes the place is haunted. It's so sad. . . ."

"Did you find out anything about what's been going on to make her think there are ghosts in her house?"

Chris shook her head. "I got the impression that Mr. Peterson didn't want to talk about it too much. Oh, Sooz, if only there was something we could do!"

"Well, maybe there is."

Chris perked up immediately. "Do you have any ideas?"

"No, not yet. But I'll think about it. Hey, speaking of ideas, how did the Halloween Dance Committee meeting go? I was so excited about B.J. that I forgot all about it. How did it go?"

"All right, I guess. It's just that I didn't quite manage to make everybody there understand my idea about making this year's dance *different*."

"Same old orange and black balloons, huh?" Susan gave her sister a teasing smile.

"As a matter of fact," Chris said, laughing, "I can practically guarantee that those will be back again this year. Oh, maybe I'm making too much of this. After all, we *are* going to have a different twist."

"Oooh, what?"

"Someone came up with the idea of having a theme for the dance. And everyone's costumes will have to fit into that theme. You know, something like space travelers or the revolutionary war . . ."

42

"Or maybe the Civil War," Susan said dreamily, remembering her fantasy of earlier that day. And it was not only the possibility of wearing a fancy ball gown that brought a smile to her lips and a glow to her brown eyes. "It sounds like a fantastic idea!"

"I suppose so." Chris made no attempt to hide her lack of enthusiasm, however. "I know it's a good idea. It's just not the kind of thing I had in mind."

She joined her sister at the kitchen table, then proceeded to tell her all about the conversation she'd had with Katy Johnson early that morning. Susan also knew Katy; she had met her through her twin, back when she, too, was in kindergarten.

"So you see," Chris finished, picking up the salt shaker and playing with it distractedly, "even though the theme idea is a good one, it doesn't make it any easier for someone like Katy to get up the courage to go to the dance alone."

Susan frowned. "I see what you mean. Well, I'll tell you what. I'll dedicate every free minute I have to trying to come up with a way to get Katy—and every other shy student at Whittington High—to that dance. Even if I have to stay awake every night from now until Halloween!

"But, in the meantime, I'd better get back to my broccoli or else we'll end up eating dinner at midnight!" She stood up and returned to the stove. Almost immediately, she began to hum.

Chris knew that making dinner for the Pratt family was not what had put Susan in such a good mood.

"Tell you what, I'll set the table," Chris offered. She went over to the cabinet above the kitchen counter and took down four dinner plates.

But as she arranged dishes and silverware on the Pratts' dining room table, it was not her task that she was thinking about. It was not the Halloween Dance, either.

43

It was B.J. Wilkins.

Could I really have misread him so completely? wondered Chris. And here I've always prided myself on my ability to understand boys!

Not that B.J. had seemed particularly difficult to understand. He certainly hadn't tried to hide the fact that he liked her—a lot. Or at least that was how it had *seemed*!

She was totally bewildered. She was also worried about her sister. If this B.J. was the type of boy who went around making every girl he met feel that she was special to him . . . well, that simply wasn't the kind of boy that Christine Pratt wanted her twin sister to get mixed up with!

But things were even more complicated than that. Not only was she confused by B.J.'s apparent interest in her and concerned over her sister's interest in *him*, she was also a bit jealous. Yes, she liked B.J., too. She couldn't deny it. And it hurt that he was interested in Susan. . . .

Enough! thought Chris. As she folded pretty green-and-white-flowered cloth napkins and tucked them underneath the knife and spoon that she'd placed at the right of each plate, she tried to reason with herself. Stop thinking about all this so much! After all, Susan can date anyone she wants—and so can B.J. You misunderstood, that's all. B.J. is probably just friendly.

She vowed not to give the matter another thought.

But as the Pratt family sat down to dinner, Susan's buoyancy was impossible to ignore. Even their parents noticed.

"What on earth is that *sound*?" Mrs. Pratt asked innocently as she helped herself to some rice. "Is someone humming? Susan, you're humming, aren't you?"

"Sorry, Mom." Susan grinned. "Guess I'm just in a particularly good mood this evening."

"That's the understatement of the year!" Mr. Pratt boomed. "I expect you to start dancing on the table any minute now! Just don't step on the biscuits. I can't stand it when there are footprints on my biscuits."

"Oh, Daddy!" Susan laughed. "You make it sound as if there's something unusual about being happy!"

"Why, not at all! But being happy is one thing and smiling at your water glass is something else altogether. Hey, wait a minute. This is just a hunch, mind you, but is there by any chance a *boy* behind all this?"

Susan just smiled secretively.

"Chris, do you know anything about any Prince Charmings that have recently arrived on the scene?"

Chris shrugged noncommittally.

"I knew it!" Mr. Pratt groaned. "Next thing you know, there'll be *five* people sitting at our dinner table. I'd better stock up on food now while I still can. Will one of you two twins please pass me some more of those delicious biscuits? I think I'll sneak a few into my pockets!"

Between her sister's cheerfulness and her father's jokes, Chris found it impossible to remain in her pensive mood for very long. By the time Susan brought out the special dessert she'd prepared, a plate of fudge brownies still warm from the oven, she was joining in with her family's laughter.

I guess you were just wrong about B.J. Wilkins, she told herself.

And she made up her mind, then and there, to forget all about him.

It never even occurred to Chris that doing just that was not going to be quite as simple as she thought!

Six

"Well, well, well. If it isn't Christine Pratt!"

Chris was standing in front of her locker, carrying half its contents in her left arm and sorting through the other half with her right, when she heard a voice behind her that sounded extremely familiar.

It was first thing in the morning, just before homeroom, and Chris hadn't quite prepared herself for coping with unexpected social encounters. Experiencing a mixture of glee, surprise, and anger, she whirled around so quickly that she nearly dropped the haphazard stack of books and papers that was balanced precariously on her arm.

"Why, hello there, B.J."

The tone of her voice sounded odd, she knew—mainly because she wasn't sure yet whether she was happy to see him or not.

He, however, appeared to have no doubts over how he was feeling about seeing her again. He was grinning from ear to ear, and his blue eyes twinkled so merrily that Chris was reminded of the jack-o'-lanterns she had noticed earlier that morning on the Petersons' porch.

Darn! thought Chris. Why does B.J. Wilkins have to be so *charming*?

"Cleaning out your locker at this hour of the morning?" he asked cheerfully. He leaned against the locker that was next to hers, acting as if the two of them were the best of friends—even though they'd only met the day before. He peered inside, then commented, "There are only a few cobwebs in there. If I were you, I'd let it go for another month or two."

Chris couldn't help laughing. "To be perfectly honest, I gave up on the idea of keeping my locker neat and organized a long time ago."

"I see. So while Christine Pratt is pretty and smart and full of good ideas about things like Halloween dances, the one area where she's less than perfect is keeping her things in order."

He was being so openly flirtatious that Chris was caught off guard.

"Actually," she explained seriously, "I'm just trying to find an old homework assignment, one I did a few weeks ago. I'm *positive* I stuck it in this locker of mine, so it's got to be here *somewhere*. . . ."

Just then, she spotted a piece of paper she hadn't noticed before.

"Here it is! Goodness, I've been looking for this for at least five minutes!" She eyed B.J. suspiciously. "Do you have magical powers or something?"

His blue eyes narrowed. In a humorous Transylvanian accent, the kind that Count Dracula always used in the movies, he said, "Now you know my see-cret! I'm not only a mind reader; I also have the power to make things appear!"

"I'm beginning to believe that! Well, now I can give this to Margie Baker. She missed the first few weeks of history class because she was originally assigned to another section. She thought that looking over the past assignments might help her to catch up."

Suddenly, Chris had an idea.

"You know, if you think this *locker* is a mess, you should see my *closet*! I wish I were more organized—the way my sister is, for example."

She watched B.J. carefully, anxious to see his reaction to what she'd just said.

But he just smiled. "Oh, yes, the *other* Pratt girl. Her name is Susan, right? And you two are identical twins. Yes, I know all about her."

Chris was taken aback by B.J.'s honesty. She wasn't sure what she'd been expecting—for him to pretend he'd never heard of Susan Pratt, or maybe for him to mention that he'd walked her home the evening before . . . But his casual attitude took Chris completely by surprise.

"So you *know* that I have a twin sister, then!"

"Of course! Why, is it supposed to be a secret?"

"Well, no . . ."

For one of the few times in her life, Christine Pratt was entirely at a loss for words.

"It's just . . . it's only that . . ."

"She's quite an accomplished artist, from what I understand. I'd like to see some of her paintings sometime."

Chris was astonished. But then she remembered her conclusion of the night before: that B.J. Wilkins was just an unusually friendly person. Even if he were planning to ask

Susan out, there was no reason why he couldn't be nice to Chris.

And then, of course, there was the possibility that he wasn't planning to ask Susan out at all, that he was just trying to make as many new friends as he could, both boys and girls. After all, he *was* new in town.

Hoping that that was the case, Chris decided to be as hospitable as she could.

"Maybe you can come over to our house one of these days and see some of Sooz's artwork."

"Yes, I'd really like to do that."

The first warning bell sounded then, startling Chris. "My goodness, it's getting late. I'd better get moving or I'll be late for homeroom!"

"I'll walk you over."

"Okay."

There it was again: that assumption that the two of them just *belonged* together. Chris couldn't remember ever having met a boy who was so self-confident right from the start. And she liked it. If only she knew what his intentions were—and whether or not she might be hurting her sister . . .

As they walked down the corridors, through the crowd of students rushing to their lockers or their homerooms, Chris and B.J. fell into a discussion of the Halloween Dance.

"You know, last night I spent the whole evening trying to think up some way to include everybody at that dance," said Chris, shaking her head slowly. "And I just couldn't come up with a single idea. I feel awful about it, too. It shouldn't be *that* difficult to be a little creative!"

"*I* know," B.J. teased. "How about making school dances a part of the Whittington High curriculum? Sort of like an extension of gym class. Then everyone would have to go."

Chris laughed. "That's a fantastic idea! Except I don't know if we could get Ms. Barlow and the other physical education teachers to agree to it.

"But here's another idea. We could put the name of every student at Whittington High into a hat and have a drawing at the end of the dance. Whoever's name was chosen would get some wonderful prize, like a television or a VCR. And the catch would be that in order to collect the prize, the winner would have to be there!"

"Terrific! Only one problem. Where would we get the money to buy the prize?"

"You've got a point." Chris sighed. "See, it's not that easy, thinking up an idea. And I really want everyone to come to that dance!"

"Well, *I'll* be there, that's for sure."

Then, in a somewhat different tone of voice, B.J. said, "You know, Chris, that dance is still a couple of weeks away, and, uh, I was wondering . . ."

"Yes?"

Chris was expecting B.J. to ask her about planning for it, something like how far in advance it was necessary to hire a band for that evening. So he really caught her by surprise with the question he did ask.

"I was wondering, how about if you and I go out together some night before then? Like this weekend, maybe. I thought maybe we could go to the movies this Friday night."

Chris was so flabbergasted that she didn't know *what* to say.

What about Susan? was the first thought that popped into her mind.

But he didn't actually *ask* Susan *out,* she quickly reminded herself. I mean, she thought he liked her and all . . . And then there's that old theory that B.J. Wilkins just happens to be a very friendly, outgoing boy.

Fortunately, they had just reached the door of Chris's homeroom. She was grateful for the chance to break off their conversation. Not that she didn't like the way it was going . . . it was just that she wasn't quite sure how to respond.

"Gee, this Friday night, huh?" she said, stalling for time. "Well, let's see. I'm not sure if I'm free then, to tell you the truth."

"Don't tell me you've got a date with somebody else!" B.J. looked genuinely disappointed.

"Oh, no, nothing like that." Chris hurried to reassure him. "It's just that, uh . . ." Her mind raced as she desperately tried to think up some excuse. "It's my parents. Yes, that's right. I think my parents wanted us all to go out to dinner together Friday night. You know, kind of a family thing. It's not definite, though, so I'll have to check."

"Okay. You do that. And let me know as soon as you're sure, all right? I've got to check with *my* folks, to make sure I can borrow the car!"

"Fine," Chris replied lamely. She didn't sound at all like a girl who'd just been asked out by a boy she really liked.

The last bell rang then, and Chris's homeroom teacher cast her a meaningful look through the open classroom door.

"I'd better run," said Chris. "And you'd better get going, too. You don't want to be late!"

"Good thing my homeroom is just down the hall."

As he started to dash off, B.J. said, "I'll be talking to you soon, Chris. And I sure hope we're on for Friday night!"

As she slunk into her homeroom and took her seat, Chris was in a daze. Once again she couldn't figure out how she felt—or how she *wanted* to feel. She liked B.J. so much, but, at the same time, she didn't understand him. One day he was walking Susan home from school, telling her he couldn't wait to see her artwork. And the very next day, he was asking Chris out to the movies!

Oh, what a mess! thought Chris, inwardly moaning. And here I was all set to forget I'd ever laid eyes on B.J. Wilkins!

Well, at least there's one thing that's perfectly clear, she thought, opening her history textbook, planning to force herself to read all about the colonization of Virginia for the entire homeroom period. There's no doubt in my mind that this time around, I am utterly, totally, *completely* confused!

Seven

Ever since Katy Johnson had confided in her about her secret crush on Wayne Lowell, Chris found herself taking a new interest in this quiet boy whom she barely knew. As she'd mentioned to her friend, he was in her third-period English class. In the past, she had never really thought of him as anything besides a pleasant-enough senior who always got *A*'s on his essays and invariably had some interesting insights to add to class discussions on the books they were reading. Now, however, she couldn't help watching him, studying him—trying to see if she could figure out what made him tick.

It's just the matchmaker in me, she thought with a smile.

Class had just started, and, for the second day in a row, she could barely concentrate on what her English teacher, Mr. Adams, was saying. Instead, she was staring at the back of Wayne Lowell's head. He sat in front of her, three seats up and two over, so she had a fairly good view of him—especially when he turned his face to the side in order to watch Mr. Adams as he paced around the classroom, his usual teaching style. Today was no exception. As he led a discussion on *Romeo and Juliet*, Mr. Adams walked up and down the aisles, talking about the great play by William Shakespeare.

Wayne was nice-looking, Chris observed, thoughtfully twisting a strand of chestnut-brown hair around her finger. He had dark hair, almost black, that was just a little bit shaggy in the back. Behind the tortoiseshell eyeglasses that he always wore, his eyes were hazel, or so she remembered from the few times she'd stood close enough to him to see them. Between his glasses, his obvious shyness, and the slightly baggy sweaters he so often wore, he reminded Chris of "the boy next door" she was always reading about in magazine stories.

She liked Wayne, but her original assessment of him, that he was one of the most bashful boys she'd ever met, still held.

Getting Wayne and Katy together is going to be one of the great challenges of my matchmaking career, Chris thought. She shook her head slowly.

"Christine, I see that you're shaking your head. Does that mean you disagree with what Tom just said?"

Mr. Adams's voice rudely snapped her back to her present situation. She was in English class—and she was supposed to be thinking about great literature, not plotting ways to get two people she really liked together.

But she hadn't been paying attention—and she'd gotten caught. Chris instantly turned beet-red.

"Uh, I, uh . . . I'm not quite sure what Tom *meant*, actually," she stuttered, hoping she sounded convincing.

"Very well. Tom, could you please rephrase the comment you just made? Then Christine will have the chance to tell us whether she agrees with you or not."

"Sure, Mr. Adams," Tom replied congenially. "What I meant was, I don't really get what the big deal about Romeo and Juliet *was*. Sure, they came from families who were enemies, and their folks wouldn't have wanted them to see each other. I understand all that. What I *don't* understand is why they didn't just see each other on the sly. You know, meet in the forest or something when nobody was around."

"An interesting point of view, Tom. Now, Christine, what do you have to say about that?"

"I think the whole thing isn't that simple. Sure, it's easy for us to judge them on our terms. But things were very different in those days. There was the question of family honor and loyalty . . . and, of course, just having the freedom to 'sneak around,' as Tom suggested.

"And, besides," she finished, a bit less certain, "if they had just decided to meet each other in secret, there wouldn't have been very much for Shakespeare to write a play about, would there?"

The entire class laughed at Chris's inventive insight— including Mr. Adams. They all had to agree that she did have a point.

But even after the class had moved on to discuss the structure of the play, the way the plot developed, and the techniques Shakespeare used to introduce his characters, Chris continued to think about what she had said—and about how romantic the story of Romeo and Juliet, the star-crossed lovers, really was.

If only that kind of thing happened these days! Two people, so much in love . . . And here I can't even get Wayne Lowell and Katy Johnson together!

And *we* have the advantage of cars and telephones, not to mention school dances!

With that, she returned to pondering the issues at hand. At the moment, the problems of Juliet and her Romeo seemed very, very far away, indeed.

By the time the bell rang to signify that third period was over, Chris had decided that she was ready to act. Perhaps the tale of Romeo and Juliet had inspired her—or perhaps she was just getting tired of feeling frustrated. At any rate, she made a point of standing right next to Wayne as the class gathered their books and shuffled out the door of the classroom into the corridors toward their fourth-period classes.

"Hi, Wayne!" she said brightly.

She hoped he wouldn't think it was *too* peculiar that, all of a sudden, she was going out of her way to speak to him.

But he didn't seem to suspect anything. Instead, he acted pleased that someone was taking the time to be friendly.

"Well, hi, Chris!"

"I'm glad that class is over, aren't you?" She rolled her eyes dramatically. "William Shakespeare is just a bit too heavy for me."

"Oh, I don't know. I kind of like his plays. At least the ones I've read so far. And *Romeo and Juliet* is such a wonderful story. It's so . . . so . . ."

"So romantic." Chris finished his sentence for him. Then she sighed wistfully. "I know exactly what you mean."

"You'd never guess it by your comments!" Wayne said playfully.

Chris laughed. "I just like to look at things realistically, I suppose. I mean, romance is great and all, but when it comes right down to it, people have to do more than just sit around and moon over each other. Daydreaming never got anybody anywhere, you know? No, sooner or later, people have got to take action!"

She paused, then went on. "Speaking of romantic things, are you planning to go to the Halloween Dance, Wayne?" Hastily, she added, "I'm on the dance committee this year, so I'm taking a special interest in the turnout."

"I don't know, Chris."

"It should be lots of fun. Even better than last year, in fact."

"Really? Why?"

"The dance committee hasn't completely worked out the details yet, but we plan to do something a bit unusual this year. What we're thinking of doing is having some kind of theme."

"What do you mean?" The tall, dark-haired boy with the round tortoiseshell glasses looked puzzled.

"We want to come up with a theme that the whole dance would be built around. You know, like animals or circus performers, or maybe a specific period in history like the revolutionary war. The decorations would be based on the idea we chose, of course, and maybe even the refreshments as well. But the main thing would be that everybody's costume would have to fit in with the theme.

"So," Chris finished, "what do you think of our idea, Wayne?"

"Gee, I don't know. I guess it sounds okay. It's *different,* anyway. But when it comes right down to it, I don't really know how I'd feel about dressing up like—like a lion, or a trapeze artist, or even a rebel or a redcoat. And getting together a costume like that sounds as if it could be pretty complicated.

"Besides," Wayne continued, "I always thought that part of the fun of Halloween was seeing how original people could be with their costumes. And seeing all kinds of different costumes: ghosts and witches and animals and clowns. You know, a little bit of everything. If there was a theme, everybody would end up looking pretty much the same, wouldn't they?"

Chris frowned. "I never thought of that."

It was true; it had never even occurred to her that some

57

people may not *want* to wear a costume that fit in with the theme that the dance committee had chosen. Or that some of them would prefer to see their classmates dressed up in a variety of getups.

Suddenly, Chris had real doubts about the entire dance idea.

But as long as she couldn't come up with anything *better,* she reminded herself, she knew it really wouldn't be fair of her to complain.

Her daydreaming about the future of the Halloween Dance was quickly cut short, however.

"Not that any of this matters to me very much, *anyway,*" Wayne was saying.

"What do you mean? Aren't you planning to go to the dance?"

Wayne cast a strange look. "Of course not, Chris. I've never gone to any of the school dances. Well, I did go to *one* once, back in the tenth grade, but I decided never to do *that* again."

"Why not? Didn't you have a good time?"

"Are you kidding? I had a *terrible* time! I went to the dance all alone, and I spent the whole evening hanging around with some of my buddies, looking at all the girls and trying to get up the nerve to ask one of them to dance." He shook his head sadly. "I never did, though, and neither did any of my friends. I guess we're all just too shy for that kind of thing.

"Anyway, that ended my interest in school dances, right then and there!"

"But that was two whole *years* ago, Wayne! Why don't you give it another try? And," Chris added, a bit more cautiously, "why don't you invite somebody this time? You know, bring a date?"

Wayne began to turn pink. "Gosh, Chris, to tell you the truth, I wouldn't know who to ask."

"Oh, come on. I bet there's *somebody* . . ."

"Well . . ."

"Listen, Wayne, your secret is safe with me. I promise not to say a word to a living soul!"

Once again, Chris simply couldn't resist the opportunity to try playing matchmaker.

"I'll tell you what: I'll give you a clue. She's without a doubt Whittington High's most outstanding female athlete."

Katy Johnson!

Chris's mouth dropped open. But before she could decide whether or not to let on that she knew precisely who Wayne was talking about, she glanced over at him and saw that the pink color of his cheeks had turned into one of the brightest shades of red she had ever seen.

"Which is one of the reasons I'd never have the courage to call her up and ask her out. I mean, why would the school's gymnastics champion want to go out with *me*?

"Besides, we hardly know each other. For all I know, maybe she doesn't even know who I am!"

Oh, she knows who you are, Chris thought ruefully. There's no doubt about that!

But she wasn't about to give Katy's secret away. After all, the girl had told Chris about her crush on Wayne Lowell in confidence. No, she couldn't be that direct, even though, at that moment, there was nothing in the world that she wanted to do more.

"Well, Chris, I've got to get going. Spanish class is next. But it was nice talking to you."

"Yes, I enjoyed talking to you, too."

It was also an extremely *educational* conversation, thought Chris.

"See you in class tomorrow, Wayne!"

"Right. And good luck with your plans for that Halloween Dance!"

As she strolled over to her next class, Chris found herself in a very blue mood. Even her worries about B.J. Wilkins—and the fact that he'd asked her for a date earlier that very same day—seemed of secondary importance.

Here the committee is putting all this planning into the Halloween Dance—decorations, music, refreshments, even a theme—and yet two people who I really like, Wayne and Katy, *still* aren't going to be there to enjoy all the fun!

There's no doubt about it, Chris thought firmly. I simply *have* to come up with something. And I'm going to . . . even if it takes every last bit of creativity I have!

On her way home from school, Chris made a point of stopping in at Petersons' Bookstore. She had been wondering about the details of poor Mrs. Carpenter's supernatural experiences ever since her last conversation with Susan about the woman's situation. She decided to try to find out more, she hoped, without Mr. Peterson figuring out what she was doing.

Fortunately, he seemed to have taken the afternoon off. Ellie Peterson, his wife, was in charge.

"Hi, Mrs. Peterson!" she said brightly as she waltzed into the store. Fortunately, there were no other customers; that would make things easier.

"Hello there, Chris. I haven't seen you for a while."

"I've been busy with school. In fact, that's why I'm here."

"Oh, really? And what can I do for you?"

Chris tried to sound matter-of-fact. "I need a book on ghosts. For a school project," she added hastily.

"Ghosts, huh? What kind of book, exactly?"

Chris was relieved; Mrs. Peterson didn't seem to connect Chris's sudden interest in spooky subjects with the recent complications with her sister-in-law. "One of those books that documents actual cases where people claimed to see them."

"You mean like in castles in England?"

"Right. And in this country, too."

"You're in luck. I have a few books on the subject that came out recently. But if you're not afraid of getting a little dust on your clothes, and maybe some cobwebs in your hair, I've got an even better idea."

With an introduction like that, Chris couldn't help being curious. "What?"

"I've got a collection of old books down in the basement. Not the kind of thing that most people want to buy or even browse through. But if I remember correctly, one or two of those are about supernatural phenomena. I think they might even refer to a few instances of supposed hauntings in this area."

A chill ran down Chris's spine. Even so, she couldn't bring herself to pass up an opportunity like this one. "Just point me in the right direction, Mrs. Peterson!"

A few minutes later, Chris was alone in the basement of the store, dodging spiderwebs—and their inhabitants—as she went through a stack of cardboard boxes, each one packed with thick, dusty old volumes. Some of them were bound in real leather and printed with gold leaf. And all of them looked impressive, as if they contained very significant information.

It wasn't long before Chris found the books Mrs. Peterson had mentioned. Sure enough, there were two books on reports of haunted houses, some of them in towns not too far from Whittington. She scanned them with interest, thinking that one day it might be fun to reread them both carefully.

And then she froze. One section, in the back of the second book, was entitled "Crabtree Hill."

Chris held her breath as she read on. For a few minutes, she forgot where she was. All she could think about was what she was reading.

In the mid-1860s, there were several reports that a ghost was seen in a cemetery in a then unsettled area, on a hill nicknamed "Crabtree Hill." Onlookers claimed that this was the ghost of Jonathan Spring, a soldier in the Civil War who had been buried there instead of with his family because he died in battle, far away from home. The legend that grew up around these sightings was that Jonathan Spring couldn't rest because he'd been buried without his loved ones, and was therefore doomed to spend eternity yearning after his parents and his sisters.

Chris suddenly felt very cold. She remembered noticing a small cemetery, a few hundred feet from Mrs. Carpenter's house, while bicycling with her sister up on Crabtree Hill a long time ago. It was so overgrown with weeds that they had only spotted it when they stumbled upon it accidentally. She hadn't thought anything of it at the time, but now it all seemed to fit in.

Maybe there really *was* a ghost living on Crabtree Hill. The ghost of Jonathan Spring.

And maybe it was *he* who was haunting Mrs. Carpenter's house!

Chris noticed for the very first time how dark, and how quiet, it was in the store's basement. It seemed so creepy . . . and she was so alone. . . . Suddenly she felt like dashing out of there, escaping from the damp cellar with its spiders and spooky shadows and book about the ghost of Jonathan Spring.

Chris grabbed the books she had been looking at and ran up the stairs, afraid to look behind her as she did.

"Find what you were looking for?" Mrs. Peterson asked congenially. And then her smile faded. "Why, Chris! You look as if you've just seen a ghost yourself!"

"Oh, um, no, Mrs. Peterson. It's just that, um, a spider was crawling down my shirt. Yes, that's it. A spider. So I ran up here to get away from it . . ."

"I told you so." Mrs. Peterson laughed. "That place hasn't been cleaned in years. But I see you found something helpful."

Chris glanced at the two dusty books she was carrying. "Uh, yes. These look as if they might be helpful. For my school project, I mean."

"Good! I'm glad someone can use them! Feel free to borrow them, Chris. Keep them for as long as you like."

"Gee, thanks, Mrs. Peterson. I think I'd better get going now, if you don't mind."

"Sure, Chris. It was nice to see you. And, as I said, I'm glad I could be of help!"

Chris ran all the way home, clutching the books to her chest so hard that there was no chance of them slipping out of her grasp. And as she went past Crabtree Hill, she kept her eyes down. For the first time in all the thousands of times she'd gone by, she was afraid that if she looked up, she might see something she'd rather not see.

Eight

As Susan was walking home from school that day, she smiled to herself when she came to the corner on which, only the day before, she had met B.J. Wilkins.

What a strange coincidence, she thought. If I hadn't been daydreaming just at the moment I was about to cross the street, and if B.J. hadn't been turning the corner at the exact same time . . .

But before she had a chance to complete that sentence, she heard the tinkling of a bell—the kind that bicyclists often use as horns. Sure enough, when she glanced up, there was B.J. on his bicycle.

This time, however, he was riding a great deal more slowly. And he was wearing a huge, playful grin.

"Hello, again!"

"B.J.!"

"Don't look so alarmed, Susan. This time you don't have to worry about being mowed down by a crazed boy on his bicycle!"

Susan laughed. "I guess you've been watching out for pedestrians with their heads in the clouds."

"Actually, there's only *one* pedestrian I've been watching out for." B.J. pulled up alongside her and climbed off his bike. "I figured you probably take the same route home from school every day, so I thought I'd take a chance and try to catch up with you. A bit less dramatically, though, this time around!"

Susan was so pleased that she didn't even care that her cheeks were turning pink.

"Well, here I am."

"If I hadn't found you, I was going to call you tonight, anyway." B.J. sounded matter-of-fact.

"Oh, really?"

"Yup. I was wondering if you were free this Saturday night. I thought you and I could go out to the movies. And," he added, his blue eyes twinkling, "maybe we could top off the evening at Fozzy's. I've heard that both their banana splits *and* their hot fudge sundaes are out of this world."

"I'd love to!"

"Great! Then we can order both a sundae *and* a banana split, and I'll have a chance to try both."

"Okay," Susan agreed with a chuckle. "I hope they have doggie bags, though, so we can bring the leftovers home. You're talking about quite a bit of ice cream!"

"I think you'll be astounded by how much I can eat. Ice cream, that is. Vegetables are an entirely different matter, I'm afraid."

"I'll remember that in case you ever come over to our house for dinner!"

"Terrific! Listen, I'll have to check with my parents to make sure I can borrow the car on Saturday night. But assuming that it's okay with them, how about if I pick you up at seven?"

Susan was already counting the hours until then.

By the time she got home, she knew that trying to settle down and get some homework done would simply be impossible. She was too excited about her Saturday-night date with B.J.

So when Chris showed up a few minutes later, Susan pounced on her immediately.

"Chris! How would you like to take that bike ride we talked about yesterday morning?"

"You mean *now*?"

"*Right* now. This very instant, in fact."

"Well, I don't have very much homework . . ."

"And it's a perfect day. Oh, please, say yes!" Susan grabbed her sister's arm and jumped up and down. "We can go over to the Atkinses' farm and get some pumpkins. Come on, it'll be fun!"

"Okay." Chris eyed her twin curiously. "Are you all right, Sooz? You're acting as if you've got ants in your pants!"

Susan just laughed gleefully. "I'll tell you all about it when we're on our way."

It was only ten minutes or so before the girls were bicycling down First Street, side by side, heading toward the road that led out of town. The Atkinses' farm, where fresh fruits and vegetables were sold almost all year round, was a few miles away, off a quiet country lane that was ideal for a long, leisurely bike ride. The girls had changed into their sloppiest jeans, and the day was just cool enough to require the pastel-colored sweaters they had both put on. It occurred to Chris that this would be a good time to tell Susan about Jonathan Spring—and the possibility that Mrs. Carpenter could be correct in her belief that her house was haunted. But it was such a beautiful day, and they were having such a good time, that it just didn't seem like the right time.

"Let's get *four* pumpkins, Chris, instead of just two," Susan suggested as they rode past the Petersons' bookstore, right in the middle of Whittington. "That way, we can give one each to Mom and Dad."

"What a great idea! And we can all carve them into jack-o'-lanterns this weekend. I think I'll make mine scary this year! He'll have the meanest jagged teeth I can make."

"Not me. I want mine to have the biggest smile in the whole wide world!"

Chris glanced over at her twin, pedaling lazily beside her. "There must be *something* behind this fantastic mood you're in today! Are you going to tell me, or do I have to guess?"

Susan giggled. "Oh, it's no secret."

"Tell me, then!"

"Oh, Chris! Remember that boy I told you about, the one I met yesterday?"

"Yes. B.J. Wilkins, right?" Chris was beginning to get nervous.

"Right! Well, I saw him after school today as I was walking home—and he asked me for a date! We're going out this Saturday night!"

Oh, no! thought Chris. But she remained silent for a few seconds.

Then, slowly, she said, "Where are you two going? To the movies, by any chance?"

"Yes! How on earth did you know?"

"Oh, just a hunch."

"Of course, it depends on whether he can get the car for that night. He has to ask his parents first before it's definite."

"Of course."

Chris was suddenly feeling rather glum.

This B.J. Wilkins is really something! she thought ruefully. Not only did he ask *both* of us out on the very same day, but he even planned the same date! And on two consecutive nights, no less!

It was all just too distressing. Chris didn't know what to do. So, for now, she decided not to do anything.

"Gee, that's great, Sooz. I hope you have a good time."

"Oh, I'm sure we will. He's so nice, Chris! I can't wait until you meet him!"

Chris tried to put B.J. out of her mind for the rest of the afternoon. Instead, she worked at concentrating on picking out the fattest, roundest pumpkins possible.

But she remained troubled. And, she knew, not thinking about B.J. wasn't going to solve anything.

Finally, that evening after dinner, when Chris had found it impossible to get any of her homework done because she was so troubled by the B.J. Wilkins business, she decided to talk to someone she considered a real authority on affairs of the heart.

"Mom, are you busy?" she asked, poking her head into the doorway of her parents' bedroom.

"No, honey. I'm just reading. Another mystery, what else?"

Mrs. Pratt was a great fan of mysteries. She had read every one in the Whittington Public Library—and even went back to reread some of the books she'd particularly enjoyed, joking that she always hoped that maybe the *second* time around, they'd turn out differently.

The book she was reading tonight, however, was one she hadn't read before. And she was finding it particularly absorbing. Even so, she readily put it down as soon as she saw the serious look on her daughter's face.

"What is it, Chris? Is something wrong?"

"Oh, no! There's nothing *wrong*, exactly. . . ."

"That's a relief. From your expression, I thought perhaps you were having some kind of problem."

"It's not *me* who's having a problem. Actually, it's—it's a friend of mine." Chris plopped down on the bed opposite the comfortable upholstered chair in which her mother was curled up with her book.

"A friend of yours?" Mrs. Pratt suppressed a knowing smile. She was only too well aware that there was no friend. "Anyone I know?" she asked innocently.

"Oh, no!" Chris's answer came too quickly. "It's someone from school. But you've never met her. I'm pretty sure of that."

"All right, then. What's your friend's problem?"

"Well, this . . . *friend* met a boy she really liked. And she was certain he liked her, too. But then—that same day, in fact—she found out that this boy had walked another girl home. Meaning that he liked *her,* too."

"Wait a minute. Is this friend of yours *sure* this boy walked this other girl home?"

Chris nodded. "Yes. The other girl told her all about it. And she went on and on about how wonderful she thinks this boy is."

"I see. The plot thickens."

"Wait, it gets even *thicker*! The very next day, this boy asked one of the girls out for Friday night, and the *other* girl out for *Saturday* night! And," she added, scowling, "he even asked both of them to go to the movies and explained that first he had to ask his parents if he could borrow their car.

"But there's even more! I still haven't told you the very worst part! These two girls happen to be . . . let's just say close friends."

"How close?"

"*Very* close." Chris paused, hoping she had made herself clear, without giving away any of the key details, of course. "Understand the problem, Mom?"

"Oh, yes. I think I understand it quite well, in fact." She wondered if Chris knew exactly *how* well she understood.

"So, what do you think she should do? I mean, do you think this friend of mine should tell her best friend that this boy is—is . . ."

Mrs. Pratt laughed gently. "What, in my day, we called a two-timer?"

"Yes, that's it precisely."

"Well, let's see." Mrs. Pratt leaned forward in her seat and folded her hands in her lap. After thinking hard for a few seconds, she put on what she hoped was an expression of great wisdom. "Chris, if these two girls really are close, I think your friend should talk to her friend about what happened."

"You do?" Chris looked at her mother in disbelief. "You don't think she should just mind her own business? Tell the boy she won't go out with him and never ever mention the whole episode again, not to her friend or to anybody else?"

"It's true that there's something to be said for minding one's own business. But it sounds as if this girl is afraid that the boy might hurt her friend. There's nothing wrong with warning her.

"And if these two girls really are such good friends, there'll be nothing lost. Just as long as she makes it clear that she's acting in her friend's best interest."

Chris thought for a few seconds. "Gee, I never really thought of it that way. I guess that if she wants to be a good friend, she really does owe it to this other girl to warn her about this boy."

Suddenly, she brightened. "I think you're right, Mom! Yes, I'm certain that you are!"

She jumped up off the bed, then leaned over and planted a quick kiss on her mother's cheek. "Thanks, Mom! I *knew* you'd know what to do!"

As she started to dash out of the room, Mrs. Pratt called after her. "Where are you going in such a hurry?"

"To talk to my friend. To call her, I mean."

"Good idea. Oh, Chris, by the way . . ."

"Yes, Mom?"

"In case you're wondering where Susan is, she's in the garage, helping your father organize his tools."

"But . . . why . . ." Suddenly, Chris burst out laughing. "Thanks a lot, Mom. You really are a peach."

Mrs. Pratt just smiled. "That's what mothers are for."

Nine

"Sooz, can I talk to you for a minute?"

Just as Mrs. Pratt had said, Susan was out in the garage with her father, pouring nails out of ragged cardboard boxes into glass jars. Both Susan and Mr. Pratt looked a bit relieved to see Chris, however.

"I was hoping for some sort of distraction," Mr. Pratt said cheerfully. "Susan and I have just put in a good hour trying to clean up this mess. I'd say it's time for a coffee break."

"Sounds like a good idea to me," Susan agreed.

To Chris, she said, "I've been wanting to talk to you, too. I'd like some advice on what to wear on my date with B.J. Saturday night. I thought maybe you'd look through my closet with me and help me pick something out."

"Funny, your date with B.J. this Saturday night is exactly what I wanted to talk to you about."

"Oh, good!" exclaimed Susan.

Chris could already tell that this was going to be even more difficult than she'd imagined.

As the girls walked upstairs together, toward the girls' bedrooms, Susan kept up a steady stream of excited conversation.

"I suppose I should just wear jeans and a nice sweater," she chirped happily. "But I'd like to look *extra* nice, somehow. . . ."

"Sooz . . ."

"Oh, I know it's not a big deal. It's just a movie date and all, but—"

"Susan, listen to me. There's something I've got to say . . ."

"I don't know, I just want it to be *special*—"

"Susan Pratt!" Chris nearly shrieked.

Susan looked over at her twin and blinked.

"Why, Chris! What on earth has gotten into you?"

Chris opened her mouth to explain, then closed it and sighed. "Look, why don't we both sit down in your room? There's something I have to tell you."

"Okay." Susan looked puzzled, but it was clear from the sparkle in her brown eyes that she was still lost in her dreamworld—at least a little bit.

Once they were comfortable in Susan's bedroom, with Chris sitting on the edge of the bed and her sister leaning back in the family's old wooden rocking chair she had latched on to long before, claiming it for her own, Chris began to speak.

"All right, Susan. Now, this is really kind of hard for me to say . . ."

"It's okay, Chris. Whatever you have to tell me, I promise I'll understand. Really!"

Susan was just beginning to realize that her sister was

being very serious about all this. Apparently she had something important to tell her, and it was something she wasn't exactly looking forward to saying.

"Well, it's about your date."

"My date with B.J.?"

Susan was surprised. What could Chris possibly know about that?

"Actually, it's about B.J. himself."

"But Chris! You've never even *met* him!"

"I'm afraid that's not entirely true."

Nervously, Chris tugged at the barrettes that were holding her shoulder-length chestnut-brown hair off her face. They were lemon yellow, the same color as the sweater she was wearing with her jeans. "You see, Sooz, I also met B.J. this week."

"You did? Where?" Susan was so curious about their meeting—and the fact that Chris hadn't mentioned it before—that she forgot to worry about whatever it was her twin was about to tell her.

"At the Halloween Dance Committee meeting."

"But Chris! That was yesterday! How come you didn't say anything before this? I mean, I kept talking about him, and . . . Well, I guess it's not really that *important*, but it *is* kind of strange that you didn't let on that you already knew him."

"There's a good reason for that." Chris tried to keep her voice even. "You see, Susan, I didn't say anything at first because I thought that B.J. was just being *friendly* to both of us."

"Well, that's possible, isn't it?"

Chris sighed. "I thought so—and I certainly *hoped* so, but . . ."

"Besides," Susan said defensively, "B.J. asked *me* out."

Chris looked at her sister soberly. "Susan, he asked me out, too."

It took a few seconds for Chris's words to register.

Susan just stared at her, without blinking, without saying a word. And when she finally did speak, it was clear that she didn't know what to say.

"But . . . when . . . if . . ." she sputtered.

"Look, Sooz," Chris said, surprising herself by how calm she sounded. "B.J. asked me out for this Friday night."

"And he asked *me* out for this *Saturday* night!"

All of a sudden, both girls started to laugh.

"That's incredible!" Susan cried. "Why would he *do* that? I mean, he must know we're twins!"

"Of course. And he must have realized we'd both find out, that we'd tell each other."

"Well, at least we know one positive thing about B.J. Wilkins."

"What's that?" Chris asked curiously.

"He's certainly consistent in his taste in girls!"

Chris and Susan burst out laughing again.

Suddenly, however, Chris grew serious once again.

"I'm glad you're taking this so well, Sooz. I was afraid you'd be upset."

"To be perfectly honest, I'm more flabbergasted than upset! I just don't understand it!"

"It's true. This B.J. Wilkins fellow certainly is a puzzle," Chris agreed. "Anyway, at first I wasn't sure if I should even tell you."

"Of course you should have! I'm glad you did! But what made you change your mind?"

Chris grinned. "Let's just say that I got some good advice from someone who's very, very wise." She paused, then asked, "So are you still planning to go out with B.J. this weekend?"

"Absolutely not! Why, I can't imagine going out with someone who would try to—try to . . ."

Chris finished her sentence for her. "To put something over on the Pratt twins!"

"Right! Now, all I have to do is decide what I'm going to say to him." Susan frowned and thought for a minute. "I think I'll just tell him the truth. That I knew he asked both me *and* my twin sister out, and that neither of us appreciate it!"

"Good idea. Let's confront him!"

Susan's eyes opened wide. "'Let's'? You mean, *both* of us?"

"Sure! Why not? After all, B.J. was willing to take on both of us Pratts before. So let's show him that we're quite a team to contend with! That we twins stick together, no matter what!"

It didn't take long for Susan to agree.

"You're on, Chris!"

Suddenly, Chris grew serious. "Sooz, there's something else I've been meaning to talk to you about."

"Oh, no! *Now* what? Don't tell me you found out that B.J. is also *married* or something!"

Chris laughed. "No, this isn't about B.J. It's about Mrs. Carpenter. And her haunted house."

Susan glanced at her sister and smiled. "Come on, Chris. You know there's no such thing as a haunted house. Why, you're the one who was telling *me* that just the other day."

Chris took a deep breath. "That was before I stumbled upon this. Here, take a look." After explaining where she'd found the book, she opened it to the place she had marked and indicated where she wanted her sister to begin reading.

"What's this? A book about ghosts? Oh, my gosh! 'Crabtree Hill'? Why, that's where Mrs. Carpenter lives!"

"Now you're catching on. Read it, Sooz."

A minute later, Susan sat back and looked at Chris. "Whoa! What's going on here? Does this mean there really *is* a ghost haunting that house?"

"I don't know, Sooz. But I *do* know that I'm dying to find out!" When her sister didn't readily agree, as she'd expected, she prompted, "Well, aren't you dying to find out, too?"

Susan eyed her twin warily. "I'm not so sure. I've never gone on a real ghost hunt before. Hey, let's look at the other book. Is there anything about Jonathan Spring in that one?"

She opened up the book, expecting to see more reports on ghosts. Instead, the pages were printed with photographs, very old-looking photographs.

"What's this? This isn't a book about ghosts."

"Oh, dear," sighed Chris. "Did I pick up the wrong book? I ran out of that basement so fast . . ."

"Chris, it's a yearbook! From Whittington High!"

"Oooh, let's see!"

The two girls pored over the old high school yearbook, a memento of a class that had graduated fifty years earlier. For the moment, ghosts were completely forgotten.

"Look at their hairstyles!" Chris shrieked. "And their clothes! They're hilarious!"

"I think they're kind of nice," said Susan. "I wonder if it was Mr. Peterson's graduating class."

"Let's look him up. The pictures are in alphabetical order."

Under the name Peterson, however, was a pretty young girl. The caption read, "Cecilia Peterson. Class Flirt."

"Look! It's Mrs. Carpenter!" Chris squealed. "Gee, she looks so young here!"

"She *is* young here," her sister pointed out. "Oh, look. Not only was she the 'Class Flirt'; she also belonged to a million clubs. Just like you, Chris."

"Yes, but she was in a sorority. Sigma Delta Alpha. She was even president during her senior year!"

"Oh, this is so exciting, being able to see Mrs. Carpenter when she was so young. And so pretty, besides!"

"Yes," Chris agreed, her voice suddenly heavy. "Who ever would have predicted that she'd end up living in a haunted house?"

Susan closed the book and sighed deeply. "Oh, Chris. What are we going to do? I'd love to help Mrs. Carpenter. In fact, now that I've seen her when she was our age, I want to help her out more than ever."

"I'd like to help her out, too. But Mr. Peterson said the other day that he'd tried everything: talking to her, reasoning with her, even offering to move into her house with his wife. She was afraid the ghosts would hurt them, though."

When she looked over at her twin, she saw that Susan's eyes had taken on a gleam that she had seen many times before.

"Uh-oh. You've just come up with an idea, haven't you?"

"I think so. Chris, how about if you and I spend the night in Mrs. Carpenter's house? Then we can see firsthand whether or not the ghost of Jonathan Spring lives there!"

"And if it does?"

Susan shrugged, suddenly matter-of-fact. "If it does, we'll tell her that she should try to get used to him."

"And if it doesn't?"

"Well, if we don't see any signs of him, then maybe she'll come to believe that he's not really there. You know, we'd be someone with an objective opinion, so we might have better luck than her brother did."

Chris was still skeptical. "This all sounds good in theory, Sooz, but there's one detail you've left out."

"What's that?"

"How do we get Mrs. Carpenter to agree to let us stay in her house overnight? She doesn't even *know* us!"

"You've got a point there." But Susan remained undaunted. "We'll just have to come up with some kind of scheme, that's all!"

"As easy as that, huh?"

"As easy as that. You don't think we could possibly ruin our track record now, at this point in our careers, do you?" Susan teased.

"I suppose you're right. Okay, then, back to the drawing board. Gee, we sure have a lot of planning to do. Coming up with a great idea for the dance, getting Katy and Wayne together—and now plotting a way to get Mrs. Carpenter to invite us over as houseguests. How do we ever get ourselves into these situations?"

Susan grinned. "That's easy, Chris. The reason we get ourselves into them is because we love getting out of them!"

Ten

The next morning, Chris and Susan did something they didn't usually do.

They dressed exactly the same.

The two girls were totally unalike in almost everything except their physical appearances. And they nearly always looked so different that it was difficult to tell that they were identical twins.

Chris tended to be flamboyant, wearing stylish clothes, fun costume jewelry, and some kind of combs or barrettes in her shoulder-length chestnut-brown hair. Her usual outfit for school was a nice pair of jeans or corduroy pants and a shirt or sweater, more often than not in a bold, cheerful color.

Susan, on the other hand, liked to wear subdued clothing. She preferred skirts to pants, especially traditional plaids or solid colors. She generally didn't bother to do anything special with her hair other than to make certain that it was well brushed and neat. And the only jewelry she felt comfortable wearing was tiny earrings or delicate neck-laces.

Today, however, was an exception.

Deciding to make a point of being sisters—*twin* sisters, at that—had something to do with wanting to present a "united front" to B.J. Wilkins.

"After all, this is *war*!" Chris exclaimed over breakfast, taking a large bite out of her English muffin in order to emphasize her point. "We need to teach this B.J. a lesson."

"Right," Susan agreed. "And that lesson is that *no* one messes with the Pratt twins!"

"Here, here," said Chris. "Especially when it comes to toying with our affections! We should nominate B.J. Wilkins for this year's 'Class Flirt'!"

So the girls both wore black corduroy pants and powder-blue sweaters. They didn't own many articles of clothing that were exactly the same, since their taste in fashion differed so widely. But these sweaters were birthday presents from their Aunt Lillian, who always sent them identical articles of clothing, sweaters or blouses or even dresses. She couldn't help it, she always said. She remembered only too clearly the days when they were little girls and their mother liked to dress them the same. Every now and then, Chris and Susan had discovered, having a set of matching clothes could come in handy.

They also wore matching combs that were supplied by Chris, and tiny gold earrings, two very similar pairs, that were supplied by Susan.

And, indeed, the two girls looked like mirror images of each other.

"There. *This* should impress B.J.," Chris said with a satisfied nod. They were about to leave for school but had stopped for one final glance in the mirror. "Having him see us both looking like the same person should make him understand the seriousness of what he's done. Imagine, trying to violate the Twins' Code of Honor."

"The *what*?" asked Susan.

Chris shrugged. "It's something I just made up. But it certainly sounds good, doesn't it?"

"Definitely. Very official. Well, even if we don't manage to impress him with how upset we both are about all this, we should at least manage to confuse him!"

Chris laughed. "All set, Sooz?"

"Ready! Let's go! At this point, I'm ready for *anything*!"

As the girls walked to school, they discussed the peculiar behavior of B.J. Wilkins, something neither of them understood yet. Chris told Susan that she was certain she would be the first to encounter him. And knowing this, her heart was pounding with anticipation as she and her sister strode purposefully through the main entrance to Whittington High.

Sure enough, just as she'd expected, Chris ran into B.J. the very first thing. As she was standing at her locker, right before homeroom, gathering her books for her morning classes, she suddenly heard that familiar voice—just as she had the morning before.

"Hi, there, Chris!" he said cheerfully, coming up behind her. "Did you find out if you're free Friday night? I checked with my parents, and it's okay for me to borrow their car."

Chris had expected to be cool and calm as she confronted him.

Instead, as she whirled around to face him, she found herself blowing up like a small volcano.

"B.J. Wilkins! Of all the nerve! Why, I can't believe you're just standing there, as cool as a cucumber, talking to me about going out Friday night as if it were the most—the most *normal* thing in the world!"

B.J. looked totally astonished. "I don't understand, Chris. What's *abnormal* about it? Besides, I thought you *wanted* to go out with me. At least that's what you said yesterday. Or did I dream the whole thing?"

"Ah, yes. Yesterday," Chris repeated. She was beginning to fume. "Yesterday was a different matter entirely. That was before I found out . . ."

"Before you found out *what*?"

Chris's brown eyes flashed angrily.

"Before I found out that you asked my twin sister out for *Saturday* night! You—you *two-timer*! Did you think we wouldn't find out you were trying to date both of us? Or was it that you simply didn't care?"

Chris was ready for all kinds of possible reactions. He could get mad. He could act as if he didn't care. Or he could get defensive, making excuses for his outrageous behavior.

The one reaction she *wasn't* prepared for, however, was the one she got.

B.J. started to laugh.

"What's so funny?" Chris demanded.

B.J. just shook his head slowly. And he continued to laugh.

Which only made Chris even *more* furious.

"Goodness gracious, what on earth is *wrong* with you, B.J.?"

"There's nothing wrong with me, Chris," he finally replied, still chuckling.

"Then go ahead and explain!"

"There's nothing to explain!"

"Aha! So you admit that you were being a two-timer, asking both me and Susan out!"

But B.J. persisted in remaining calm. "I'm not admitting anything. *Least* of all that I've done anything *wrong*."

Chris's mouth dropped open.

"B.J. Wilkins," she cried, "you're even *worse* than I ever imagined!"

He looked at her innocently, with his blue eyes open wide.

"Gee, Chris, does this mean our date for Friday night is off, then?"

Chris just let out a yelp of total exasperation. Then she stomped off, slamming her locker door behind her.

As she stalked away, B.J. just stood there. And he was still chuckling.

I have never *ever* in my entire life met anyone like this boy! Chris thought, hurrying away. For once, she was actually glad that it was time for school to start for the day.

Susan's experience with confronting B.J. wasn't very different from Chris's.

She ran into him right after second period, as she was coming out of math. He was waiting for her, right outside the classroom.

"Hey, Susan! Over here!"

"B.J.!"

Susan was caught totally off guard; she hadn't expected to run into him this early in the day. Yet it appeared that he had made a point of finding her.

"How did you know where I'd be during second period?"

B.J. grinned mischievously. "I'm a mind reader, remember?"

When she didn't laugh, however, when she just stood there, staring at him in an odd manner, he immediately became more serious.

"Actually, it was just a lucky coincidence. I was walking by just now, since my gym class let out a little early, and I happened to glance into this classroom and saw you sitting there, right in front."

"We seem destined to keep running into each other by accident."

"It must be fate," he said, smiling again. He looked as if he didn't have a care in the world. "Well, I just wanted to tell you that I checked with my parents, and it's okay if I borrow the car this weekend. So we're definitely on for Saturday night."

"Wait a minute. Not so fast."

B.J. finally noticed that something was wrong. At least as far as Susan was concerned.

"Uh-oh. What's up? Is there something else you have to do instead on Saturday night? If you can't make it, we can always try again next weekend."

"*Next* weekend! B.J., you are the lowest, most ruthless, most—most—"

"Susan! What's the matter?" The expression on B.J.'s face was one of genuine astonishment.

Susan's eyes narrowed angrily.

"Let me tell you something, Mr. B.J. Wilkins! If you think you can pull the wool over the eyes of the Pratt twins, then think again! Chris and I *both* know exactly what you're up to!"

"And what is it that I'm up to?"

"Imagine, asking us both out. And for the same weekend, no less! Chris on Friday night, me on Saturday night . . . Why, I've never heard of anything like it before, not in my entire life!"

"Oh" was all that B.J. said.

"'Oh'? '*Oh*'? Is *that* all you have to say?" Susan demanded.

"Well, no. I'd also like to say that I think I'm beginning to understand the problem here."

"It's not that difficult to understand. You're nothing but a—a *two-timer*, and you've been caught!"

When B.J. started to laugh, Susan could hardly believe what she was seeing.

"I don't think it's funny!"

"I do. In fact, I think it's *very* funny!"

"Oh, really? Then does that mean you're ready to explain what it is you think you're doing?"

B.J. thought for a moment. Then, calmly, he said, "No, I don't think I'm ready to explain anything right now."

"Probably because there *is* no explanation. You're just— you're just . . ."

"Low, and ruthless, and—wait, I've forgotten what else it was you called me."

Instead of looking as if he was sorry, or even embarrassed by having been caught at his little game, B.J. simply looked amused. He was still smiling, in fact. And that only made Susan even more angry—and even more frustrated.

"You really don't care at all, do you? Tell me, did you react the same way this morning when Chris confronted you, when she let you know we were on to you? Did you just stand there, laughing like what she was telling you was the funniest thing you'd ever heard in your life?"

"Uh, well, to tell you the truth—"

"And did you notice that she and I are dressed the same today?"

"Actually, I *didn't*."

"We were making a statement. We wanted to impress upon you the fact that we're sisters. *Twin* sisters. We tell each other everything. And we have no intention of letting some—some *boy* come between us!"

So what if B.J. didn't notice that Chris and I were dressed the same, thought Susan, trying not to be too disappointed that their little ploy, designed to have an extra bit of impact, had failed. *Telling* him about it was almost as good.

Not that it really mattered. Not anymore. As of this moment, she was officially washing her hands of one B.J. Wilkins.

As if to symbolize the importance of the moment, the bell suddenly rang.

"Oh, dear," Susan moaned, "now I'm going to be late for my next class!"

But all B.J. said was, "So I guess that all this means we won't be going out Saturday night, after all."

Susan just gasped.

"B.J. Wilkins!" she cried. "You . . . are . . . *incorrigible*!"

With that, she turned on her heel and flounced away.

What a strange, horrible boy, Susan thought as she raced down the hall. She broke into a run, partly because she wanted to get to her third-period class, partly because she wanted to get away from B.J. I can hardly wait to compare notes with Chris. I wonder if her confrontation with him went any better than mine did?

Fortunately, Susan and Chris were getting together for lunch that day. And lunch period was now only an hour or so away. Susan knew she would find out soon enough.

And she couldn't wait to hear every single detail.

Eleven

"*And* then *he said, 'Gee, Chris, does this mean our date for* Friday night is off, then?'*"

"You're kidding! That's exactly what he said to me! He said, 'So I guess that all this means we won't be going out Saturday night, after all.'"

Chris and Susan were sitting together in the Whittington High School cafeteria, filling each other in on the details of each of their separate confrontations with B.J. Wilkins. They had made a point of choosing a table in the back corner of the huge room, which was filled with students who chattered away, happily and loudly, as they ate their lunches. Usually, both Chris and Susan used the lunch period as a chance to do exactly the same thing. But today they wanted to discuss the boy who had been monopolizing both girls' thoughts for almost all of the past forty-eight hours. And they wanted plenty of privacy in which to do it.

"Isn't he amazing!" Susan exclaimed, once each twin

had told the other every word of the short conversation she'd had with B.J. "He didn't even *care* that he'd been caught red-handed!"

"It's worse than that," said Chris. "He actually *laughed* when I told him. He laughed! As if the whole episode were the funniest thing in the whole world!"

"And he didn't even try to offer any explanation."

"How could he? There *is* no explanation!"

"Except, of course, that he's someone who simply doesn't believe in playing fair." Susan put her chin in her hands and leaned her elbows on the table.

"To think that we both liked him so much! We both thought he was so *nice*!"

"Well, he managed to fool us both, that's all. He's what's known as a 'smooth operator.'"

"Well," said Chris, "at this point, I have only one thing to say to Mr. B.J. Wilkins."

"What's that?"

"Good riddance!"

With that, she picked up her cheeseburger, part of the school lunch she had just bought, and bit into it. Susan, who had brought her lunch from home, reached into her brown paper bag and pulled out a sandwich.

"Oooh, he makes me so mad," Chris muttered as she chewed.

"I thought we weren't going to talk about B.J. anymore," Susan reminded her. "Listen, let's just have a nice, quiet lunch, okay? You eat your cheeseburger, and I'll eat my peanut butter and jelly sandwich. Hey, look, there's Katy Johnson! Why, I haven't talked to her . . . well, at least since the beginning of school this year."

Susan waved to Katy, then gestured toward the empty chair next to her once she'd caught her eye. With a nod, the redheaded girl headed toward their table, lunch tray in hand.

"Hi, Katy! Why don't you join us for lunch?"

"Thanks, Susan. The only thing is, I can only stay for a few minutes." She smiled at the twins apologetically. "I promised Ms. Barlow I'd spend the second half of my lunch period talking about some new ideas she has for a routine I'm trying to put together before our next meet. But if you don't mind if I eat and run, I'd love to."

"We understand completely. Here, pull up a chair."

Katy set her tray on the table and sat down next to Susan.

"This is a real coincidence, you know," said Susan. "I was just telling Chris that I haven't seen you since the beginning of the school year."

"Funny, I was talking to Chris about the same thing just a couple of days ago."

"Of course," Susan went on, "that doesn't mean I haven't been reading about you in the school paper. In the Whittington *Herald*, too, I might add. You're really getting quite a reputation as an athlete!"

"Maybe the Olympics are in Katy Johnson's future!" Chris was only half-teasing.

"Oh, come on, you guys." Predictably, the modest gymnast was blushing, reluctant to be in the spotlight once again. "Listen, why don't you come to our next meet? I could use a little moral support while I'm trying out my new routine. A couple of friends in the audience, cheering me on, wouldn't hurt!"

"You're on!" cried Chris. "That is, if we can manage to get through the crowds of your adoring fans."

One of whom just happens to be Wayne Lowell, thought Chris. But she decided not to say anything about Wayne. At least not yet.

After she had rearranged the food on her lunch tray, Katy

suddenly looked at Susan more carefully. She looked over at Chris, and then back at Susan again.

"What's going on with you two?" she asked, blinking hard as she looked at them both one more time. "Or am I seeing double?"

"What do you mean?" Chris asked, surprised. But then she remembered that she and her twin were dressed the same way today—something that even Katy, who rarely saw them anymore, recognized as unusual.

"Oh, you mean the mirror-image bit." Chris sighed. "It's a long story. Let me just sum it all up by saying that Sooz and I were trying to teach a particular boy we both know a lesson."

"I see. And did it work?"

Susan and Chris exchange woeful glances.

"I'm afraid not," said Susan. "But I guess you can't win 'em all."

Chris decided it was time to pounce.

"Speaking of boys," she said, suddenly displaying more enthusiasm than she had since she sat down to eat, "I was talking to Wayne Lowell the other day."

"Oh, really?"

Katy sounded so casual that it would have been obvious to anyone that something was up. Not wanting to embarrass her, Susan pretended she was so busy trying to get the clear plastic wrap off her peanut butter and jelly sandwich that she didn't have time to listen to what the other two were talking about.

"What's new with Wayne?" Katy asked in that same tone of voice.

"Nothing much. We were just talking about how romantic the play *Romeo and Juliet* is. We're reading it in Mr. Adams's English class."

"Oh, yes. It *is* romantic. Such a beautiful, sad story."

A dreamy look came into Katy's eyes. Susan recognized it as the same one that came into *her* eyes every time she thought about *Gone With the Wind.* Thinking of that reminded her that she hadn't yet gotten around to asking her mother to help her make a Civil War–style ball gown for the Halloween Dance. She'd simply been too busy shopping for pumpkins, helping her father clean the garage, and day-dreaming about B.J.

"Well, we *did* talk about other things," Chris went on.

"Oh, really? Like what?"

Now Katy was pretending to be busy putting ketchup on her cheeseburger. Chris and Susan exchanged amused glances.

"Oh, like the Halloween Dance."

"That's nice. Is he planning to go?"

"Not unless he's got a date." Chris hesitated, wondering if she should tell Katy *everything* that Wayne had said. But she decided against it. After all, he had told her about his crush on Katy in confidence. She couldn't betray his secret—even though she wanted to match them up together so badly that she felt as if she were about to burst.

Before she could drop a few hints, however, Katy innocently asked Susan how her drawing and painting were going, and the other Pratt girl launched into a detailed monologue on the two art classes she was taking that semester. The moment had passed, and Chris had no choice but to drop the subject.

But that doesn't mean I'm going to forget it, Chris thought, gobbling down three french fries at once.

After a few more minutes of conversation, during which Susan, Chris, and Katy filled each other in on what they'd each been doing lately, Katy suddenly stood up.

"Well, this has been a lot of fun. I'm glad we had a chance to talk, but I really do have to run."

"I know. It's hard work being a celebrity," Chris teased.

"Maybe we should get Katy's autograph *now*, Chris," Susan added, "while we still have a chance."

"You two!" Katy laughed. "As if having *one* of you around weren't enough . . . Anyway, let's get together again soon, okay? Hopefully, for a longer visit!"

"Definitely. And let us know whenever you feel like going for that bike ride we talked about!" Chris called after her.

After Katy had left, Chris turned to Susan and sighed.

"Katy's such a nice girl," she said sadly. "If only I could match her up with Wayne Lowell . . . And if only I could use the Halloween Dance to do it. I mean, it's so close! It's a little more than two weeks away! It would be the perfect time to get them together."

"Poor Chris!" Susan shook her head sympathetically. "You've been trying so hard to come up with an original idea for this dance. It really is too bad it's such a difficult thing to do. But I guess that sometimes it's just not possible to get involved in other people's lives. You know what I mean, Chris?"

But it was obvious to Susan that her twin wasn't listening to a word she was saying.

Instead, she was staring at Susan's lunch. And there was a very peculiar look on her face.

"Sooz," she suddenly asked, sounding very serious, "what kind of sandwich is that?"

"It's peanut butter and jelly, on white bread. Why?"

"Peanut butter and jelly," Chris repeated. From the expression on her face, it looked as if she had just found, in that phrase, all the secrets of the universe.

"Peanut butter and jelly!" she cried once again. "Don't you understand, Sooz?"

93

"Gee, no. I'm afraid not. But you're certainly welcome to half my sandwich, if you want it."

"Peanut butter and jelly." Chris said it one more time. Her brown eyes were glowing in a way that her twin had never seen before.

"Here, *take* it, Chris. Take the whole thing. Really, I'm not that hungry, and—"

"Romeo and Juliet," said Chris. She looked as if she were a million miles away. "Mickey Mouse and Minnie Mouse. Prince Charles and Princess Di. Napoleon and Josephine. *Now* do you get it?"

Susan was trying hard not to lose patience with her sister. "Christine Pratt, you are making absolutely no sense at all! Will you please calm down and tell me what on earth you're *talking* about? Romeo and Juliet, peanut butter and jelly . . ."

"Don't you see? It's our gimmick for the Halloween Dance! Our way of getting everybody to participate, whether they have a date or not!"

By this point, Susan had given up entirely on any hopes she had ever had of finishing her lunch. Her peanut butter and jelly sandwich, the one that had started it all, was pushed away and quickly forgotten.

"I'm all ears," she said with a loud sigh. "Please explain, O Strange One."

"Oooh, this is the brainstorm of the century!" Chris was so excited that she was actually jumping up and down in her seat. "You see, everybody at Whittington High will be given a slip of paper with the name of one half of a famous duo written on it when they buy a ticket for the dance.

"Take Romeo and Juliet, for example. Whoever gets assigned Juliet has to dress up like that and go to the dance. Then, when she gets there, she looks for Romeo. And she automatically has him as her date for the evening!

"Don't you see? No matter how shy somebody is, there'll still be someone there to dance with! This plan guarantees a date for everyone!"

Susan thought about Chris's idea for a few seconds. She had to admit that it wasn't bad.

"But what if someone already *has* a date?" she asked. "If a boy and a girl were looking forward to going to the dance together, they'd be pretty disappointed if each of them got assigned to somebody else."

"That's easy. If two people are already paired off, they'll automatically get matching halves."

"I see," Susan said. "You mean when people go to buy tickets, they just say whether they want to be matched up with someone or go as a ready-made pair."

"Exactly! It's like a blind date, kind of, but much more fun!"

"Wait. There's something else I'm not clear on."

"What's that?"

"Well, it's true that your original idea was to come up with something that would encourage everybody to go to the dance, either with or without a date, but what about Katy and Wayne? I mean, I don't see how this idea would manage to get them together. If they decide to participate, the odds that the two of them will get both halves of a matching pair are slim."

"Ah," said Chris, her eyes twinkling devilishly, "that's where my being on the dance committee comes in."

"You mean you would pull strings in order to make sure the two of them were paired off?"

Chris just smiled.

"But that's not exactly playing by the rules . . . is it?"

"Where matchmaking is concerned," Chris said firmly, "there are no rules. Haven't you ever heard that expression, 'All's fair in love and war'?"

95

"That's a pretty convincing argument." Susan laughed.

"So, Sooz, do you think I've got something here?"

"Oh, definitely! I think your idea is utterly fantastic!"

"Me, too! I mean, at the risk of sounding as if I'm bragging . . . Gee, I can't wait to tell the rest of the dance committee about it! Oh, I hope they all like it!"

"I'm sure they will."

Susan hesitated for a moment, then said, "Hey, Chris?"

"Yes?"

"What if some people already have costume ideas in mind?"

"Hmmm. That could be a problem."

But it was one that Susan solved as quickly as she had brought it up.

"I know! Say I wanted to go as Scarlett O'Hara. Which I do, as a matter of fact. When I go to buy my ticket to the dance, I'll tell the person in charge to make sure to assign someone the character of Rhett Butler. That way, I'm guaranteed a partner, but I'll still have the fun of not knowing who he is until I get there!"

"That's the perfect solution. I'll make sure to include it when I tell the Halloween Dance Committee all about my idea. Hmmm . . . Maybe we should even schedule an emergency meeting." Chris's brain was already ticking away. "I usually see Betsy Carter between sixth and seventh periods. . . ."

"How about you, Chris? Are you going to plan a costume, or would rather be surprised?"

"Oh, I don't know. I guess it would be sort of fun to be surprised . . . although, come to think of it, there *is* one person it might be fun to dress up as. Someone it would be fun to be for an entire evening."

"Really? Who?"

Chris's answer was the last one that her twin would ever have expected.

"Juliet."

"You mean, as in *Romeo and Juliet*?"

"None other. What do you think?"

Susan laughed. "I think that you and I have a lot of sewing to do over the next week or two!"

The two girls launched into a happy discussion of Chris's clever idea—and the costumes they planned to make. It was clear that they were both enthusiastic about the new twist the Halloween Dance would be taking, once the Halloween Dance Committee approved it.

The one question that neither girl dared to ask, however, was one that was very much on both of their minds.

What would happen if B.J. Wilkins somehow got assigned to be either of the girls' other half?

Finally, the two girls lapsed into silence for a few seconds. Susan started to take advantage of this break to resume eating her lunch. She reached for her peanut butter and jelly sandwich—and then stopped.

"Chris, I just had a brainstorm of my own. You're not the only one who's on a roll today."

Chris glanced up from her cheeseburger. "Really? Something about the dance?"

"No, this is about something entirely different. I just had an idea about how we can get ourselves into Mrs. Carpenter's house. And, if we play our cards right, spend the whole night there."

Now, Chris's lunch was also forgotten. Her brown eyes began to gleam—just as they always did whenever she was on the verge of embarking on some new adventure. "Fantastic! I knew you would! What's your idea?"

"Well, remember what it said in that yearbook you found in the basement of Petersons' Bookstore? That Cecilia

Peterson, as she was known then, was the president of that sorority?"

"Right. I remember. It was called Sigma Delta Alpha."

"Well, that sorority is our ticket to Crabtree Hill!"

Chris sighed impatiently. "Susan Pratt, what on earth are you talking about?"

"Listen. You and I show up at Mrs. Carpenter's door one night and tell her that we want to join Sigma Delta Alpha, and we're going through the initiation."

"I get it! Hazing, right? But that sorority doesn't exist anymore!"

"For heaven's sake, Chris, Mrs. Carpenter won't know that! *Anyway,* since she was president when she was in high school, she should feel some sense of loyalty to good old Sigma Delta Alpha, right? And so she'll be willing to help us."

"Go on."

Susan shrugged. "It's simple. We'll just tell her that as part of our hazing, we have to spend the night at her house, since it's supposedly haunted."

Chris's jaw dropped open. "Susan, that *is* a brainstorm! Oooh, if only she believes it!"

"I think we can manage to be convincing. After all, we've always been pretty good at that sort of thing in the past. There's only one problem."

"What's that?" Chris was puzzled.

Susan had suddenly become very serious. "Oh, nothing much. Just that you and I are about to spend an entire night, right before Halloween, sleeping in a haunted house!"

Twelve

At Chris's suggestion, Betsy Carter scheduled a special meeting of the Halloween Dance Committee for the following afternoon.

Chris had butterflies in her stomach as she walked into the biology lab, where, once again, the meeting was being held. She was more excited about her idea than ever, and in the day and a half that followed her original inspiration, which she had gotten during lunch with Susan, she had planned out every last detail in her own mind. She had even gone so far as to make a long list of every famous duo she could think of: historical couples, characters from books and plays, movie stars. She had even included peanut butter and jelly.

What she was worried about was successfully describing her idea to the rest of the committee, in a way that would make them as enthusiastic about it as she was.

So she was actually nervous as she took her seat. And

noticing that B.J. Wilkins was sitting at the back of classroom again, grinning in her direction, didn't help her butterflies.

"Okay, let's get right to the point," Betsy Carter began, taking her place at the front of the room. "We called this special meeting because one of you came up with an idea for the Halloween Dance that's entirely different from what we discussed at the meeting on Monday.

"Personally, I think it's spectacular. But the committee should vote on it before we decide to go ahead with it. And if we do, it'll take a lot of planning. We'll need these few extra days to put the whole thing in gear."

"Hey, I hope this 'new idea' doesn't mean I won't be able to go to the dance dressed as a man from Mars," called out Don Ellis.

"I thought that was how you were dressed today, Don," Connie McCormick teased.

Betsy laughed along with everyone else in the room, including Don.

"Don't worry, Don. If you feel that strongly about being a man from Mars, we guarantee that you'll be able to. But why don't I stop talking and let the originator of the plan describe the whole thing in detail? Chris, come on up to the front."

Once she was facing her audience, Chris forgot all about being nervous. She was too involved in what she was saying. As she launched into a description of her plan, all she cared about was making it sound as exciting as she was convinced it was.

"Well, I've given this year's Halloween Dance a lot of thought," she began. "Of course, I wanted to come up with an idea that was fresh and original—something along the lines of having a theme, the idea we came up with last time.

"But I wanted the dance to be even more than that. I wanted to think of some kind of gimmick that would let all the students at Whittington High participate, whether they had dates or not."

She hesitated, taking a moment to look each member of her small audience in the eye. "And I think I finally came up with something. I call it 'Masquerade for Two.'"

For the next ten minutes, Chris talked without stopping. She explained her plan, then went on to discuss every detail: the assignment of one-half of a famous duo at the time a ticket to the dance was purchased, a few days in advance of the dance itself; couples who wanted to come as a pair; people who wanted to wear a particular costume—as both she and her sister did.

"For example, I want to go to the dance dressed as Juliet," she told the other committee members. "And my twin sister, Susan, wants to be Scarlett O'Hara. So when we go to buy our tickets next week, we'll tell the ticket seller to make sure that some boy gets assigned Romeo, and some other boy gets assigned Rhett Butler."

When she was certain she had covered everything, Chris finally paused. "So, there's the plan for Masquerade for Two, in a nutshell. Now, are there any questions?"

"Wow, that's really something," Don commented. "I'd say your idea is inspired."

"*I'd* say it's ingenious!" cried Connie. "Chris, you're a mastermind! I *love* the Masquerade for Two!"

For the first time since she'd walked in the door, Chris relaxed.

"I'm so glad you like it, Connie," she began. "You, too, Don—"

But Betsy interrupted her. "I have a feeling *everyone* likes it, Chris. Why don't we take a vote?"

Once again, she took her place at the front of the classroom. Chris, meanwhile, sat down.

"All in favor of going with Chris's idea of Masquerade for Two, raise your hands."

The vote was unanimous.

"Then it's settled."

As if it needed to be in writing in order to be official, Betsy scrawled "Masquerade for Two" across the blackboard.

"Now, let's get down to the nitty-gritty details. We've still got a lot of work ahead of us!"

For almost an hour, the dance committee went over every single aspect of the dance—not only dealing with the matching of two halves, but also the refreshments, the music, and the decorations. By the time everyone on the committee had been assigned two or three tasks to complete before the next meeting, early the following week, Chris was satisfied that this Halloween Dance would, indeed, be the best one Whittington High had ever had.

As the meeting was breaking up, Chris was lost in thought about one of the tasks she'd been assigned: expanding upon the list of famous duos that she'd already started.

I'll enlist Sooz's help, she decided. And Dad's and Mom's as well. I bet they'll have lots of good ideas. In fact, we can all try to think up famous duos as we're carving our pumpkins into jack-o'-lanterns this weekend.

"Congratulations!" she suddenly heard a familiar voice say.

Instantly, she was snapped out of her daydreaming. She turned and found herself face-to-face with B.J.

"I really like your idea, Chris," he said cheerfully. "It's super! I'm glad the committee voted to go ahead with it."

"Gee, uh, thanks, B.J."

Since their conversation the day before—and its abrupt ending—she wasn't quite sure how to act. In fact, she was a bit surprised to see that they were still on speaking terms!

"I'm glad the committee liked it, too. I was so afraid they'd vote it down! I would have been terribly disappointed."

"You know, you're really something, Christine Pratt."

By now, the biology lab was empty, and the two of them were alone together. Even though B.J. sounded amazingly matter-of-fact, Chris suddenly felt self-conscious. She looked at him, surprised.

"Why, thanks, B.J. But I'm afraid I'm not sure what you mean."

"Well, not only are you considerate enough to be concerned about making sure that *everybody* feels comfortable coming to the Halloween Dance, especially when no one else even gave it a thought. But you're also clever enough to come up with a solution to the problem. I really admire that."

"Gosh, I . . ." Chris was so flabbergasted by B.J.'s flattery that she didn't know what to say. Or even how to react, for that matter.

"Listen, I know that this week hasn't exactly been the *smoothest* week in the world, as far as you and I are concerned." B.J. grinned. "But I was wondering. How about if you and I let bygones be bygones and go to that Halloween Dance together? You can even choose the costumes we'll wear. If you want to be Juliet, I'd be more than happy to be your Romeo."

"B.J.!" Chris shrieked. "Didn't you hear a single *word* I said yesterday?"

"Well, sure, but—"

"I have absolutely no intention of going to the Halloween Dance, or anywhere else for that matter, with a—a *two-timer*!"

She picked up her schoolbooks and flounced away, making a beeline for the door.

"Hold on a second, Chris. You know, you're not giving me a fair shake."

Chris stopped in her tracks and whirled around. Her mouth dropped open in amazement.

"Oh, really? And can you give me one good reason why I should?"

B.J. thought for a moment. "Believe me when I tell you that there *is* a reason, and a very good one, at that. I'm really not such a bad guy, you know. But you'll find out what I'm talking about soon enough. On the night of the Halloween Dance, in fact."

"What are you talking about?" Chris demanded. She was losing her patience.

"You'll see. But, in the meantime, just do me one favor."

"What?" Chris asked warily.

"Promise me that you'll dance with me that night, okay?"

"Well, I suppose I can manage *that* much." Even though she agreed, she was still reluctant.

"Terrific. For old times' sake. See? I *told* you you were something else!"

Chris just gave B.J. a strange look.

She still wasn't sure why she was agreeing to dance with him . . . except that one dance certainly couldn't hurt anything. And, besides, he was being so darn mysterious!

"You know, I'm only saying yes because I still want an explanation from you, B.J."

104

"Oh, you'll get one. The night of the dance. You've got my word on that."

There was a mischievous glint in B.J.'s blue eyes.

As she strode out of the room, more uncertain than ever about what was going on, he called after her.

"Just wait, Chris. Halloween is always full of surprises. And I'm not exaggerating when I say that, this year, you'll be getting more tricks and more treats than you've ever expected!"

Thirteen

"The terrible two-timer strikes again!"

As soon as Chris got home that afternoon, after the Halloween Dance Committee meeting had ended and she had had still one more bewildering conversation with B.J., she rushed upstairs to her sister's bedroom. Just as she expected, Susan was sitting at her desk, putting the final touches on a watercolor she'd been working on for several days. It was just one of the paintings she was getting ready for her portfolio of artwork that she planned to submit when she applied to art schools.

But when she heard her twin behind her, Susan immediately placed her paintbrush in the glass of water that was on the desk, exactly for that purpose, and turned around in her chair.

"Oh, no," she groaned. "*Now* what? Although I'm almost afraid to ask!"

Chris plopped down on the twin bed, kicked off her

shoes, and pulled her feet up so that she could sit cross-legged.

"We had another meeting of the Halloween Dance Committee after school today. You know, the special one that Betsy scheduled so that I could tell everyone about my idea. Did I tell you I'd named it Masquerade for Two?"

"Yes, yes, I know all about that," Susan interrupted impatiently. "And I want to hear all about the meeting. But first, tell me about B.J.!"

"Okay. I'm getting to that. After the meeting, he came over to me to say how much he liked my idea and how glad he was that everyone voted for it. Oh, guess what, Sooz? The committee's vote in favor of Masquerade for Two was unanimous! We're definitely going ahead with it!"

"That's great, Chris. Go *on*!"

"All right, all right. Anyway, after we talked about that for a few minutes—and, frankly, I was kind of surprised to find that B.J. and I were even on speaking terms—"

"Christine Pratt! If you don't tell me what B.J. said within the next thirty seconds, I'm going to come over there and paint your face Cerulean Blue!" Susan retrieved her paintbrush from the glass of water and waved it about threateningly.

"Sooz," Chris said, leaning forward dramatically, "B.J. actually had the *nerve* to ask me to go to the Halloween Dance with him! As his date!"

"No!"

"Yes!"

"Are you sure you understood him correctly?"

"Susan," Chris said evenly, "B.J. said he would be happy to be Romeo if I wanted to be Juliet. Could anything possibly be more clear than that?"

"I'm—I'm speechless!" Susan breathed. She deposited her watercolor brush back into the water glass once again.

"I can see that. But aren't you going to ask me what I told him?"

"What did you tell him?"

"Well, *no,* of course. Although I did agree to dance with him."

"Chris!"

Chris shrugged. "I figured one dance couldn't hurt anything. Besides, you can dance with him, too."

"He hasn't asked me to."

Chris gave her twin a peculiar look. "At this point, wouldn't you be surprised if he *didn't*?"

"You've got a point there. I'm definitely beginning to see a trend in his behavior." Susan sighed. "Did he say anything else?"

"As a matter of fact, he did. Something rather mysterious, now that you mention it."

"What?" Susan's brown eyes opened wide.

"He said that there's a perfectly good explanation for his behavior—or something along those lines."

"Oh, really?" Susan sounded skeptical. "And did he tell you what that explanation is?"

Chris shook her head. "Nope. He said I'd find out the night of the Halloween Dance."

"Uh-oh. It sounds like B.J. is up to something."

"Now that you mention it, Sooz, he *did* say that I'd be getting more tricks and more treats than I'd ever expect."

The twins just looked at each other for a few seconds.

And then, all of a sudden, the same mischievous glint came into both girls' eyes.

"Sooz, are you thinking what I'm thinking?" Chris's voice was almost a whisper.

"I think that's a definite possibility, Chris. That is, if you're thinking that it might be time for the Pratt twins to pull a few tricks and treats of their own!"

"That's precisely what I was thinking. If B.J. has some kind of prank in mind for the night of the Halloween Dance, it's only fitting that we beat him to the punch!"

"Especially since you and I have lots of experience in that area!"

"That's right. It's not easy for someone to get the best of us, once we put our minds to it!"

"And I'd say it's time for us to put our minds to it!" Susan was growing more and more excited. "Oooh, I'd love to get back at B.J.! And what better time than Halloween? Now, all we need is an idea."

Chris looked at her twin and grinned.

"Sooz, remember what I was saying the other day about the mysterious effect that pumpkins have on people?"

"Of course. The Pumpkin Principle. You said that there's something about pumpkins that makes people want to dress up like someone other than who they really are and pretend to *be* that person. And now that you've brought it up, I think I'm beginning to understand what kind of 'trick' you've got in mind!"

"At the meeting today, I mentioned that you were planning to go to the Halloween Dance dressed as Scarlett O'Hara and that I wanted to go as Juliet."

"So everyone expects us to wear those costumes. Everyone, including B.J. Wilkins!"

Chris's brown eyes were glowing. "Sooz, how would you feel about pulling a switch?"

But instead of the enthusiastic reception that Chris expected to get from her twin, Susan's face fell.

"But Chris! I wanted to be Scarlett O'Hara so badly! It's like a dream come true!"

"I know." Chris frowned. "And I wanted to be Juliet. But, after all, there's a principle at stake here. I mean, we *are* trying to fool B.J."

"That's true. He did try to fool us, in a way, and I'd love to turn the tables around and fool him, instead." She still sounded uncertain, however.

"Me, too. So, do you think it's worth it? Giving up the chance to be Scarlett O'Hara just so we can teach B.J. a lesson?"

Susan thought for a minute. She sat with her chin resting in her hands, and she wore an earnest expression. And then, suddenly, she broke into a huge grin.

"There's no question about it, Chris! As much as I'd love to be a Southern belle for the evening, I can't resist the opportunity to play a prank! *Especially* on B.J.! And since we can almost bet on him pulling some strings and getting assigned either Romeo or Rhett Butler, I can't think of a better way!"

"That's the old Pratt spirit!"

"Speaking of 'the old Pratt spirit,' " said Susan, suddenly serious, "don't forget that tomorrow night's the night you and I are going up to Crabtree Hill, hopefully to spend the night."

"As if I could forget! It's all I've been thinking about ever since we decided to go ahead and do it. But we'd better give some thought to what we're going to tell Mom. After all, if all goes well, we'll be away all night. And we also have to plan what we're going to say and what we're going to wear. . . ."

The two girls had been so absorbed in talking that they didn't even hear their mother calling them from downstairs. When Mrs. Pratt finally appeared in the doorway of Susan's room, puzzled about the lack of response to her repeated calls, it was almost a full minute before the twins even noticed that she was standing there.

"What are my two little urchins up to *this* time?" She laughed when the girls looked up and saw her. "I could be wrong, but it sounds as if you're planning another one of the pranks you're getting so famous for. Talking about 'what you're going to wear.' Don't tell me that, once again, it's going to become impossible for me to tell which of my very own daughters is which!"

The girls looked at each other, wondering just how much of their conversation their mother had overheard. But she didn't seem to have any inkling of the escapade up on Crabtree Hill that they were getting ready for. Instead, they decided to concentrate on talking to her about the Halloween Dance.

"Don't worry, Mom," Chris reassured her. "We may have a teensy-weensy practical joke up our sleeves, but we promise that you don't have to worry. As long as we're in this house, I'll continue to be Chris and Susan will be Susan."

"Wait a minute, Susan," Susan said, unable to resist the opportunity to tease their mother. "I thought that *I* was Chris and *you* were Susan!"

"You two!" Mrs. Pratt laughed. "All I can say is, I'm glad you didn't turn out to be triplets!"

"Wow," Chris breathed. "Triplets. I never even thought of that. Now *that* would have been really something!"

"Fortunately, it's too late for that," said Mrs. Pratt, sounding genuinely relieved. "And it's going to be too late for dinner, as well, if you two don't get yourselves downstairs before your father eats up all the spaghetti."

"Oh, yum!" Chris cried, jumping up off the bed. "I love spaghetti!" She turned back to her sister and mother, having decided not to dash out of the bedroom and down to the dinner table just yet. "Do you suppose Juliet ate a lot of spaghetti?"

"Not if she wanted to fit into her Halloween costume," Susan teased.

111

"Oh, that's right: Halloween *is* getting close, isn't it?" Mrs. Pratt observed casually. "I hadn't given it much thought. Have you?"

Chris and Susan both burst out laughing.

"You could say that, Mom," said Chris.

"As a matter of fact, we were both just talking about our costumes for the Halloween Dance. . . ."

"And we were wondering if maybe you could find the time to help us make them."

"Just as long as you don't want to be bunny rabbits again," returned Mrs. Pratt, rolling her eyes upward for effect. "I'll never forget the year we had fuzz all over the house. Why, even at Christmastime, I was *still* finding little clumps of white fur in the oddest places!"

"Oh, Mom, we were eight years old then!" Susan squealed.

"Really? It seems like only yesterday to me!"

"Actually," said Chris, "our costume ideas are much more interesting than that."

"And I bet they're a lot more complicated."

"Well, maybe just a little. You see, one of us wants to be Juliet, as in *Romeo and Juliet,*" Susan explained, "and the other wants to be Scarlett O'Hara."

"Oh, dear. That does sound complicated. But certainly manageable." Mrs. Pratt paused. "Did you notice that I didn't even ask which one of you wanted to be which character? See, I'm learning!"

As the three of them went downstairs together, Mrs. Pratt suggested, "How about if, right after dinner, we all drive over to the mall and pick out some fabric. If I'm going to help you both turn into two of the most beautiful—*and* well-dressed—women in the history of literature, we'd better get moving right away!"

Mrs. Pratt had never seen a spaghetti dinner eaten quite so quickly in her entire life.

112

Fourteen

"That full moon sure looks eerie, doesn't it?" Chris observed nervously.

It was the following evening, right after dinner, and Chris and Susan were heading toward Mrs. Carpenter's house on Crabtree Hill. They were walking briskly, pretending it was because it was cold. In reality, they were going so fast because they were both very nervous.

Susan glanced up at the sky. It was a black, cloudless sky, without a single star. The only light came from the round, yellow moon, which did, indeed, look eerie.

"Oh, come on. It's just the moon. The same old moon that's up there every night." Now that they had embarked on their adventure, she wasn't about to let on how scared she was. After all, she reasoned, what good would that do?

"I guess you're right," Chris agreed meekly.

"Do you think Mom believed us when we said we'd be spending the evening at Katy Johnson's and that we'd probably be sleeping over at her house?"

"I guess so. I mean, she let us go, didn't she?"

Susan was quiet for a minute. "Gee, I feel so bad about not being able to tell Mom the truth."

"I understand that, Sooz. But think how bad you'd feel if Mrs. Carpenter gave up her home, and we just stood by and let it happen without doing anything to prevent it!"

"You've got a point there." Susan sighed. "Well, I guess I'd better stop worrying about *this* world and start thinking about the possibility that tonight, you and I might be facing someone from the *other* world!"

It was as if the seriousness of what they were about to do had just hit them. They stopped in their tracks and looked at each other. Both pairs of big brown eyes were wide open.

"Are—are you scared, Chris?"

"Nah, I . . . well, sure, Sooz. Don't tell me you are, too. You're always so levelheaded, so—so *practical*."

"Maybe. But ghost hunting has nothing to do with being practical!"

The two girls continued their walk up Crabtree Hill, leaving the buildings and lights of Whittington behind. But instead of the energetic pace they had begun with, they were now proceeding much more slowly.

"You don't want to turn back, do you?" Chris finally said, her voice almost a whisper. "We could always tell Mom that Katy wasn't home."

At that suggestion, Susan suddenly became indignant. "Christine Pratt! Where's your sense of duty? You and I are about to do a good deed for a very nice woman who happens to be the sister of the owner of our favorite bookstore. How can you even *suggest* turning back?

"Besides," she added, much more calmly, "Jonathan Spring was probably a very friendly fellow during his lifetime. So there's no reason to believe he's anything but friendly *now*, right?''

Chris remained silent.

"Right?" Susan repeated.

Her twin gulped. "Anything you say, Sooz."

By that point, the girls had reached the black wrought-iron gate that marked the entrance to Crabtree Hill. Just beyond it, the huge Victorian house loomed up ahead. It was impressive, indeed: a complicated collection of towers, stained-glass windows, gingerbread trim, and turrets, with a widow's watch perched on top.

Once the house had been a grand lady. Now it was badly in need of another coat of yellow paint. The lawn was scraggly, sprinkled with patches of brown dirt where grass refused to grow. The front porch sagged badly.

And off to one side, the girls knew, was the cemetery. The place where Jonathan Spring had been buried more than a hundred years before.

B.J. Wilkins had been right. The house *did* look haunted.

"Well, this is it," said Susan, taking a deep breath. "Let's go."

The two girls went up the front walk and onto the porch. Chris glanced at her sister as if to say, "It's still not too late to go back," then reached up to the brass knocker and banged as hard as she could.

From within came nothing but silence. *Ghostly* silence.

"Maybe she's moved out already. . . ." But before the words were out of Susan's mouth, the front door opened with a loud creak. Standing there was Mrs. Carpenter, whom the twins recognized from seeing her in town.

"Mrs. Carpenter? I'm Susan Pratt, and this is my sister Christine. We're friends of your brother, Mr. Peterson, and

115

his wife, Ellie, too. We have, um, sort of a favor we'd like to ask of you."

"Yes, girls? What is it?"

"We're pledging for a sorority. Maybe you've heard of it. It's called Sigma Delta Alpha."

The gray-haired woman's face lit up. "Why, yes! As a matter of fact, when I was your age, I was president of Sigma Delta Alpha! What can I do to help you two?"

"Well," said Chris, looking over at her twin for support, "as part of our hazing, we've been told that we have to, um, spend the night in your house." She held her breath, afraid of what Mrs. Carpenter's response might be.

But the older woman simply looked concerned. "My goodness! Don't you girls know this house is haunted?"

"Yes, ma'am. At least, that's what we've heard." Susan was matter-of-fact. "That's the whole idea. You know when someone is pledging for a sorority, she has to do all kinds of things—sometimes even scary things. Which is why we're supposed to spend the night here." She noticed for the first time how terribly dark it was up here on Crabtree Hill without any streetlights or lights from other houses.

"And if we *don't* spend the night here," Chris piped up, "we won't be able to join Sigma Delta Alpha."

"We'd be *so* disappointed if that happened!"

Mrs. Carpenter thought for a few seconds. "I'm not sure about this, girls. I'm not convinced that it's safe for *anyone* to stay here."

"Oh, please!" Chris cried. "It would mean so much to us!"

Cecilia Carpenter was taken aback by her vehemence. "Well, if you're sure you're not frightened, I don't suppose it would matter *too* much if you both slept in the living room, where there are two comfortable couches and a fireplace. It's the only place that's warm enough, I'm afraid. The rest of the house gets very cold—except for my bedroom, where there's another fireplace. I'll be up there, on the third floor, so you won't bother me a bit. But are you *sure* you're not afraid?"

"We're sure!" the twins exclaimed in unison. In fact, they were so intent on convincing Mrs. Carpenter that she should let them in that they forgot to be scared.

It wasn't until a while later, when the three of them sat down to tea, that the girls remembered their true purpose in coming to this house. They were seated in the living room, which suited the exterior of the house perfectly: thick, red velvet drapes, an elaborate Oriental rug, and heavy, old furniture made of dark wood and upholstered in the same red velvet as the drapes.

"Just sitting in this room gives me the creeps!" Chris whispered to Susan while Mrs. Carpenter was out in the kitchen preparing their tea.

"Actually, this is rather a nice surprise," Mrs. Carpenter said once she'd returned. She poured tea from a silver urn into delicate porcelain cups hand-painted with pink roses. "I don't get much company these days. Tell me about yourselves."

The twins were self-conscious at first, talking to Mrs. Carpenter. But she seemed genuinely interested in finding out more about them, and, before long, they launched into hilarious tales of the little schemes they had cooked up in the past—and the predicaments they'd gotten themselves into. Mrs. Carpenter laughed along with them, and she seemed to be having a very good time.

It was past ten when she finally said, "I've enjoyed getting to know you two. But it's getting late, and I'm afraid I really must get to bed. I think you'll be comfortable on these couches. I do feel I must warn you, however. There is definitely a ghost in this house. Especially in this room."

"I've been meaning to ask you about that," said Susan. "Have you actually *seen* it?"

"Well, no. But I've heard it. I used to sleep on the first floor, in the bedroom right behind this room. And every night I'd be awakened by all kinds of terrible noises. Doors slamming, stairs creaking, books and things being toppled off shelves and tables. But the worst is a kind of high-pitched sound. It sounds like screaming." Mrs. Carpenter shuddered. "It's enough to make your blood run cold."

"Did you ever get out of bed to have a look?" asked Chris.

"Goodness, no! I was afraid of what I might see!"

Chris could certainly understand *that*.

"But I know I'm not imagining these noises because every morning, I find signs that they've been here."

"Like what?" Susan blinked.

"Chairs that have been tipped over, papers and bottles of ink that have been thrown off the desk, pillows tossed off the couch. Whoever this ghost is, he certainly isn't very neat."

The twins would have laughed if Mrs. Carpenter didn't look so distressed over the whole thing.

"If you're still prepared to stay here overnight—and very possibly see this ghost for yourselves, right in this room—then I'll be going up to bed now. There are some blankets in the hall closet." Mrs. Carpenter stood up and headed for the stairway. "And girls?" she said, turning back for a moment.

"Yes?"

"If you're not still here in the morning, I'll understand why you've left."

118

With that, Chris and Susan were left all alone.

"Gee, Sooz. Did you hear Mrs. Carpenter's description of all the noises she's been hearing? They certainly sound real enough!"

"And they couldn't very well be just her imagination if she's been finding chairs and books on the floor the next day."

As the two of them looked at each other, they were thinking the exact same thing.

"Come on, Chris. We've come this far. We can't turn back now."

"I suppose you're right. Well, we might as well find some blankets and get comfortable." Looking at Susan, her face glowing eerily in the firelight, Chris added, "I have a feeling we have a long night ahead of us."

Not long after the girls had drifted off to sleep, they both awoke with a start. The floorboards were creaking very softly. Someone—or something—was in the room with them.

"Chris, is that you?" Susan called, her voice barely audible. By then the fire had died out, and the room was completely dark. "Are you walking around?"

"No," came Chris's shaky reply. "I'm still lying on the couch. I was hoping it was *you* who was walking around."

Susan inhaled sharply. "I guess we're not alone, then."

The two girls lay in the dark, keeping very still, afraid to move. Sure enough, they began hearing the noises that Mrs. Carpenter had described. The stairs creaked, doors slammed, things fell to the floor.

"Gosh, Chris! It's as if this house were *alive*!" Susan whispered hoarsely. "I've never been so scared in my life!"

"Me, either! Oooh, we should have left a light on." Chris was actually trembling.

119

"Can't you see ghosts even in the dark? Don't they glow or something?"

Just then there was a loud crash. It sounded as if something—a vase or maybe a ceramic pitcher—had fallen onto the floor and broken into a thousand pieces. Both girls let out a loud squeal.

"Let's get out of here, Sooz!"

But something had changed Susan's reaction from fear to anger. Maybe it was the fact that Mrs. Carpenter's lovely things were being destroyed; maybe it was the fact that this kind woman was being forced out of her house. At any rate, she decided that it was definitely time to get to the bottom of all this.

"No, Chris. I'm getting up. I'm going to turn on a light. I want to get a good look at the ghost of Jonathan Spring, once and for all!"

With that, she jumped up and pulled the chain on the ornate lamp that she remembered was right next to the couch. She blinked a few times as her eyes struggled to adjust to the bright light that suddenly flooded the room.

And then she burst out laughing.

"There are our ghosts, Chris! And they don't look anything at all like Civil War soldiers!"

Chris, who had had the blankets pulled up over her head, peeked out, still not quite ready to see what had been "haunting" the house on Crabtree Hill.

"Cats!" she cried. "They're not ghosts; they're cats!"

Sure enough, when the twins checked around the living room, they found a small opening in the wall near the front door. Five stray cats who probably spent their days prowling around the cemetery were sneaking into the house at night, probably to get warm. And as they ran around in the dark, they were bound to knock things over.

"Oh, Chris, I can't *wait* to tell Mrs. Carpenter! She'll be so relieved to find out that it's nothing more than cats who are haunting her house. This means she can stay here after all!"

"All she has to do is cover up that hole. So much for the ghost of Jonathan Spring! I feel like waking her up right now and telling her who the real culprits are."

"I have a better idea," said Susan. "Let's tell her first thing in the morning—over breakfast in bed.

"But, for now, let's get these ghost-cats out of here. You and I deserve a good-night's sleep!"

Fifteen

"Oh, girls, how can I ever thank you enough?"

It was early the next morning. Mrs. Carpenter was propped up in her bed, enjoying the breakfast of French toast that Chris and Susan had prepared for her and delivered to her bed—along with a report on what they'd discovered about her "ghosts." And she couldn't have been more delighted.

"Are you still planning to move out?" Chris teased. "Because if you are, I know a bunch of cats who may be interested in buying your house."

Mrs. Carpenter laughed. "Sorry, but this house is not for sale! But, seriously, I would like to do *something* for you girls. To thank you for your bravery, your perseverance . . . and your creativity in coming up with that story about Sigma Delta Alpha!"

"I have an idea," said Susan. "It may be too much to ask, but . . ."

"Anything. Anything at all."

"Well, I've been thinking. Last night, after we'd discovered what was making all those mysterious sounds and went back to bed, I couldn't fall asleep for the longest time. I kept thinking about those poor cats. They don't have a real home. That's why they have to scavenge around and sneak into people's houses at night for warmth. And it occurred to me that since they're already used to living up here on Crabtree Hill—"

"Susan Pratt!" her twin exclaimed. "Are you asking Mrs. Carpenter to adopt five stray cats?"

"Why, I think that's a lovely idea," said the older woman, pouring a hefty serving of maple syrup over her French toast.

"You *do*?" both twins cried.

"Well, except for one small detail. I can see keeping *four* cats, but *five*? That would make things a bit crowded, don't you think?"

"But what would you do with the fifth cat?" asked Susan.

Mrs. Carpenter just smiled.

"Oooh, I'd *love* to have a cat!" Susan broke into a huge grin.

"We'll have to convince Mom and Dad that it's a good idea," Chris reminded her. "But I'm willing to help you do that on two conditions. One is that we can share him. And the other is that you let me name him."

"All right," Susan agreed. "Do you already have a name picked out?"

"You bet," Chris said seriously. "I'm going to name him Jonathan!"

* * *

For the next two weeks, Susan and Chris put all their energy into getting ready for Halloween. They carved their pumpkins from the Atkinses' farm into jack-o'-lanterns, came up with almost two hundred famous duos for the Masquerade for Two, and planned every last detail of the dance. And they spent every spare moment they had working on their costumes, drawing upon Mrs. Pratt's creativity as well as her sewing expertise.

Throughout all their preparations, the twins never lost sight of their goal: to play a Halloween "trick" on B.J.— and to have as much fun as they could doing it. They were relieved that neither of them ran into him very often in the meantime. Somehow, that just made the prospect of fooling him on the night of the Halloween Dance that much more delicious.

And then, finally, the day they had been waiting for so anxiously arrived. All that Friday, neither twin could think about anything else. Listening to a lecture on the human body or participating in a class discussion on *Hamlet* was simply impossible. After all, that would have required concentrating on something other than the look they both expected to see on B.J. Wilkins's face once he realized that the girls had switched identities—and, as a result, he couldn't be sure *which* Pratt twin he was dancing with!

Their excitement on the evening of the dance did not go unnoticed by their father.

"My goodness!" Mr. Pratt exclaimed, holding a forkful of mashed potatoes suspended in midair. "Did they just announce on the radio that food is going out of style? Or is there some kind of contest going on here that I haven't heard about? Something like a pie-eating contest, maybe, where whoever eats dinner fastest wins a trip to Paris?"

"Oh, Daddy!" Susan laughed. "Chris and I are just in kind of a hurry tonight."

"That's the understatement of the century! Do you mind telling me why? Or would I have to be a twin in order to be privy to such a secret?"

"It's no secret," said Chris. "Tonight's our school's Halloween Dance, that's all. And we're anxious to start getting ready for it."

"Oh, I see. So that explains why you two have been running around with pincushions and petticoats for the last two weeks. See, I do have *some* sense of what goes on around here! Even so, I think I'd better put seconds on my plate right now while I still have the chance. I have a feeling that, before you know it, we'll have moved on to dessert!"

But tonight, neither Susan nor Chris had the patience to waste time with dessert.

They dashed upstairs the moment they'd finished dinner. Immediately, they began to fix their hair, put on their makeup, and finally, just before it was time to leave for the dance, don their costumes.

"Well, Sooz, what do you think?"

The two girls were standing in front of the full-length mirror in Chris's bedroom looking over the two literary characters they had just transformed themselves into.

Susan examined both their reflections for a few seconds before answering her twin's question. Just as they'd agreed two weeks earlier, Chris was dressed as Scarlett O'Hara and Susan was Juliet. Then, with an approving nod, she said, "I think we both look pretty fantastic!"

And she was right. Chris was convincing as a beautiful Southern belle, and with her coloring, she did indeed look very much the way that Scarlett O'Hara was described in *Gone With the Wind*. Her chestnut-brown hair was pulled back on both sides with lavender satin ribbons tied into tiny bows. Her earrings were tiny pearls that dangled ever so slightly from a fine gold chain. And her makeup, while not unusual, was much more dramatic than she ever would have worn it. Ruby-red lipstick, a generous dusting of pink blush, and four thick coats of mascara.

The most outstanding feature of her costume, however, was undoubtedly her ball gown. It was the same shade of lavender as the ribbons she wore in her hair, and the fabric had the same satin sheen to it. It had full puffed sleeves and a round neckline, and it fit snugly from the waist up.

As for the floor-length skirt, it billowed out so far that Chris couldn't even put her arms down at her side. It had required yards and yards of fabric, as well as the construction of two hoops, one at the hips and one at the hem, to support it.

Both the girls and their mother had spent hours wondering how the women who had really worn that type of dress ever managed to get around, much less do something as simple as sit in a chair! Even though Chris expected that it would be great fun to wear a dress like this one for an evening, she had to admit that she preferred the simplicity, comfort, and ease of mobility that jeans and knee-length skirts allowed.

Making the costume was a lot of work, but all three agreed that it was worth it. Chris looked lovely, just the way the twins had always imagined that Scarlett would look. She even had a sparkle in her eyes that was similar to the one that the feisty heroine was surely meant to have.

As for Susan's costume, it was equally romantic, although in an entirely different way. Her dress was made of rich purple velveteen. It had long sleeves, a high neckline, and a tight-fitting bodice. The skirt, also floor-length, swirled down gently, the velveteen falling into soft folds. At the hem, neck, and cuffs was gold brocade trim, which gave the entire dress a very medieval look.

Susan's makeup was similar to Chris's. And her hair was left to flow freely. On her head, however, she wore a tiny cap made from the same purple velveteen and gold trim, and styled after one that was typical of that period, according to a photograph they found in the encyclopedia.

All in all, Susan's assessment was one hundred percent correct. The girls *did* look fantastic.

As the twins were admiring their costumes in the mirror, they were startled to hear a knock at the door. They assumed it would be their mother, coming to catch one final glimpse of her miraculous handiwork before the girls left for the dance.

Instead, it was Mr. Pratt.

"You know," he said, looking a bit sheepish, "I was only teasing before when I acted as if I didn't know that you girls were going to a costume party tonight. As a matter of fact, on my way home from work tonight, I stopped off and got you these. As sort of a finishing touch."

From behind his back, Mr. Pratt pulled out two long-stemmed roses. Bowing before his daughters, he presented each one with a flower.

"Oh, Daddy, they're gorgeous!" Susan cried.

"And they're perfect for our costumes!"

"Well, I knew tonight was special, and I thought I'd try to make it just a little bit *more* special." He kissed each girl on the cheek, then said, "You both look beautiful. And I think there's even a lesson to be learned here."

"What?" the girls asked in unison.

"That you two can have a good time *without* playing tricks on anyone. Pretending to be each other, trying to fool people . . . all those mischievous little pranks you've both played in the past."

The twins just looked at each other and smiled.

By the time they reached the school gym, where the Halloween Dance was being held, the festivities were already well underway. Even Chris, who had had a hand in planning the decorations and the other details, was surprised—and impressed.

The gym had been entirely transformed. It was now a dungeon, with black walls, eerie lighting, and frightening touches in the least-expected places: a low-flying bat hanging from a basketball hoop, a ghost behind the coatrack, green-faced goblins jumping out of nowhere. There were black and orange balloons and streamers, but there were also jack-o'-lanterns with glowing faces, real haystacks, and even a skeleton swaying next to the refreshment table.

"Oooh, this is better than I ever imagined!" Susan squealed. "Why, even though I must have been in this gym a thousand times, I'm actually scared!"

Fortunately, the loud rock music, performed by a band whose members were all Whittington High School students, reminded them that they were there to dance and have fun—not to cower in fear.

"Notice anything else unusual?" Chris yelled over the music.

"Well . . ." Susan surveyed the room. It didn't take her long to realize exactly what her sister was talking about.

"Wow! This is quite a turnout! And I've never seen so many people dancing together before at *any* of our school dances!"

It was true; the dance floor was packed. The only students

who were standing on the sidelines were doing so because they were talking to their friends or gulping down cider, powdered doughnuts, and pumpkin-shaped cookies. The usual groups of boys, and corresponding groups of girls, who stood together, watching without actually taking part, simply were not a part of this school dance.

Chris nodded. She looked a bit smug—and Susan couldn't blame her one bit.

"And what *else* do you notice, Sooz?"

Susan looked more closely at the people who were dancing. Every couple was dressed as a famous duo! She immediately spotted Napoleon and Josephine, Tom Sawyer and Becky Thatcher, Popeye and Olive Oyl.

One particular couple, however, had Susan entirely mystified.

"All these famous couples! But there's one I just can't figure out," Susan said. "Look at those two, Chris. What— or who—are *they* supposed to be?"

Chris looked over in the direction in which Susan was pointing. She saw a girl dressed entirely in purple: purple tights, purple sneakers, a purple sweatshirt with a purple hood. Even her face was painted purple. And her dancing partner was dressed similarly except that he was entirely in tan. He wore tan pants, a tan shirt, and a tan hat.

"That's easy," Chris replied with a chuckle. "I know *exactly* what they are."

"What?"

"Peanut butter and jelly!"

After the girls had stopped at the refreshment table for a cup of cider, they decided to split up. That way, B.J. Wilkins—probably dressed as either Rhett Butler or Romeo—would be able to find his "other half," dance with her . . . and then discover that he'd been tricked.

129

It wasn't long before Susan noticed that a boy dressed in striped pantaloons was making a beeline in her direction. He was wearing a mask over his face so that his true identity was concealed. But she knew exactly who he was.

Uh-oh, thought Susan. Here comes Romeo! Get ready. It's time for me to turn on my Chris personality.

"Juliet, may I have this dance?" the boy asked politely once he'd reached her. His voice was muffled by his mask, but she had no doubt that he was B.J. Wilkins.

Susan quickly became so involved in dancing that she didn't notice that, across the gym, the same scene was being repeated.

Chris, standing over by the refreshments, saw a boy heading in her direction. His costume was a gray Civil War uniform, the type worn by the Confederate soldiers. He, too, was wearing a face mask, one with a thick black mustache on it. It was easy to tell that he was none other than Rhett Butler.

"Miss Scarlett," he asked with a thick Southern accent, "may I have this dance?"

Chris just nodded, then whirled onto the dance floor with him.

During the entire dance, each girl was waiting anxiously for the right moment to pounce—to reveal that she was not the twin that her dancing partner thought she was. But the music was too loud, and the dance floor was just too crowded.

Once the dance was over, the twins automatically began to look for each other. Now that they had actually danced with B.J., they had both decided, it was time to reveal their prank.

At almost the same time, Chris and Susan spotted each other and began making their way across the gym, their dancing partners in tow. When Chris saw that her sister had Romeo with her, and Susan saw that her twin was with Rhett Butler, both were astonished.

Finally, the girls reached each other. The foursome stood together: Chris, Susan, and the two masked boys.

And then something entirely unexpected happened.

"Thanks for the dance, Ms. Pratt," the boys said at the same time.

With that, they pulled off their masks.

The boys grinned.

Susan and Chris gasped.

There were *two* B.J. Wilkinses!

"B.J.!" cried Chris. "What . . . who . . ."

"Wait a minute," Susan interrupted. "Which one of you is B.J.?"

"Would you believe that we're *both* B.J. Wilkins?" said Romeo, his blue eyes twinkling with glee.

Susan and Chris just looked at each other. They were so astounded that they didn't know what to do. Or say. Or even *think*!

"Perhaps we should introduce ourselves," said Romeo. "My name is Robert Wilkins. Also known as B.J. After all, everyone calls me Bob, and my middle name is James."

"And I'm William Wilkins," said Rhett Butler with a smug smile. "Also known as B.J., since everyone calls me Bill, and my middle name is John!"

"They're *twins*!" Chris and Susan cried in unison.

"You guessed it." Bill laughed.

"I don't believe it!"

"We've been tricked!"

"Don't say I didn't warn you," said Bob. "Well, I warned Chris, anyway. By the way," he teased, "you *are* Chris, aren't you?"

131

"How—how did you *know* we were going to switch costumes?" Chris demanded, still flabbergasted by the realization that there were not one, but *two* B.J.'s.

"Remember who you're dealing with," Bob replied. "You know the old expression, 'It takes one to know one'? Well, you two aren't the only set of twins in the world! And you're not the only ones who've taken advantage of being identical to play tricks on people!"

"So I see!" By this point, Susan had gotten over being shocked. She started to laugh, too.

"Well, Chris," she said. "It looks as if someone's finally beaten us at our own game!"

"I'll say," Chris agreed. "Why, I had no idea! It never even occurred to me . . ."

"That's funny. It didn't even occur to us to try to fool you until you were both so indignant that the same boy—or who you *thought* was the same boy—asked you both out," explained Bill. "You see, it all just started out as a coincidence. I met Susan after school that day when I nearly ran her over with my bicycle. And when I got home, Bob started telling me about this girl *he'd* met that day named *Christine* Pratt. For some reason, it never even dawned on us that you'd both think we were the same person!"

"Well, you *do* use the same name," Susan said. "That's enough to confuse anybody!"

"That's from when we were little," said Bill. "Our mother used to say that she couldn't tell us apart . . . and, of course, we weren't about to make things any easier for her! I'm sure you two understand all about that! Anyway, the solution she came up with was to start calling us both B.J., and, well, it just sort of stuck."

"So, Chris," said Bob, turning to Scarlett O'Hara, "was I right about our little 'trick or treat'?"

132

"Definitely! I'm willing to admit that the Pratt twins have finally met their match!"

"Well, I'm just glad that there are enough Pratt girls to go around," said Bill. "And to pick up where all this began: Susan, may I have this dance?"

"An excellent idea," Bob agreed. "Chris, how about it?"

And so it was that two very oddly matched couples joined the crowd on the dance floor. Rhett Butler was dancing with Juliet, and Romeo was dancing with Scarlett O'Hara. And all four shared a delightful secret: that underneath the makeup and the masks, there were really two identical couples dancing together.

Sixteen

"Well, Sooz," said Chris with a grin, "I guess the Pratt twins and the Wilkins twins are two of a kind. Or should I say 'four of a kind'?"

"It was only a question of time until we got beaten at our own game," returned Susan. She laughed, then added, "You know what this means, don't you?"

"No, what?"

"That from now on, you and I will simply have to work *harder* at coming up with even more clever—and more outrageous—pranks!"

After dancing for more than half an hour, the two sets of twins had finally stopped to catch their breath. They stood next to the refreshment table, helping themselves to cider and powdered doughnuts.

"I don't know about your future as mischief-makers," teased Bill, Susan's date for the rest of the evening, "but if you ever decide to go into the party-planning business, I'd say you've got it made. This is one terrific Halloween dance!"

"It certainly is," Bob agreed. "Are the Whittington High School dances always this packed?"

But before either of the girls could answer, Bill interrupted.

"Well, Bob, old boy, there's only one way to find out. We'll simply have to make sure we come to the *next* dance. So we can compare, of course. And I don't know about you," Bill went on, "but I already know who I want my date to be." He looked over at Susan fondly.

"Me, too." Bob, not to be outdone by his twin brother, reached over and took Chris's hand. "As for the rest of *this* dance, I plan to dance every dance with Scarlett O'Hara here. That is, if Miss Scarlett agrees."

"Oh, yes," said Chris. "Even though we're a most unlikely pair! I mean, whoever heard of Romeo dancing with Scarlett O'Hara?"

"Speaking of pairs, look who's over there." Susan grabbed her sister's arm, then pointed over toward the dance floor.

There, dancing together, were Peter Pan and Wendy. But their disguises, as clever as they were, did not conceal their true identities.

"Oh, yes. There's Katy Johnson and Wayne Lowell."

"You don't sound very surprised," Susan observed. She was taken aback by her sister's lack of enthusiasm.

But Chris's brown eyes twinkled merrily. "To be perfectly honest, I'm not. After all, I was determined to match up Katy and Wayne, even if it meant pulling a few strings."

Bill and Bob exchanged glances.

"Gee, I can't imagine *anyone* doing that!" Bob pretended to be horrified.

"How exactly did you managed to make sure that Katy was assigned the character of Wendy and Wayne was assigned Peter Pan?"

"Easy." Chris shrugged. "I just told Connie McCormick, who was in charge of selling tickets, to make sure they were paired off together."

"Why, speak of the devil. Here comes Connie now!"

Connie, dressed as Raggedy Ann and followed by a boy the twins didn't know but who, in his Raggedy Andy costume, was obviously her other "half," was heading in their direction.

"Oh, Chris! *There* you are!" Connie rushed over, looking extremely forlorn. "Listen, Chris, I'm *so* sorry!"

"About what?"

"That I couldn't match up those two friends of yours! I intended to, but I was out sick last Thursday. And, wouldn't you know it, that happened to be the day they bought their tickets for the dance!"

"Are you sure, Connie?"

"Well, I *think* so. I mean, I know for certain that they didn't buy their tickets any of the other days. I was on the lookout for both of them, and neither of them ever showed up."

"But . . . then how . . ."

Chris and Susan just looked at each other and blinked. They were both totally puzzled.

"If Connie didn't match up Katy and Wayne," Chris mused, thinking aloud, "then how on earth . . ."

It didn't take her long to find out.

A minute or two later, when the band stopped to take a break, Katy and Wayne headed over toward the refreshments. They immediately noticed the twins, standing close by with their dates for the evening.

"Hi, Chris! Hi, Susan!" Katy called gaily.

"Hi, Katy. Are you, uh, having a good time tonight?"

"Oh, yes, Chris! In fact, I wanted to thank you. You and the rest of the Halloween Dance Committee did a fantastic job this year. This is a wonderful dance!"

"I'll say," Wayne agreed. "Boy, this was a great idea, matching up two halves of a famous couple."

"And I heard about what you two did to help out Mrs. Carpenter," Katy went on. "However do you find the time to *do* all these things?"

"I guess we do keep pretty busy," Chris admitted. "And these days, we have one more thing to do: make sure one of us feeds Johathan every night!"

"Jonathan?" Katy repeated. "Who's that?"

Chris and Susan looked at each other and laughed.

"One of the ghosts that haunted Crabtree Hill," said Susan. "But he's retired now, and he's spending all his time being a professional pussycat."

"Wayne," Chris said suddenly, "would you please get me another doughnut? I'd ask Bob here, but, well, I've already had him go back to the refreshment table for me twice."

When Bob started to protest, Chris cast him a warning look.

"Sure, Chris," said Wayne. "I'd be happy to."

As soon as he was gone, Chris pounced on her friend.

"Katy Johnson, how on earth did Wayne ever get up the courage to ask you to this dance?"

"He didn't," the red-haired girl replied matter-of-factly.

"But I know for certain that you two weren't assigned matching halves. I tried my best, but—"

"Why, Christine Pratt! You didn't!"

Chris blushed. "Well, I knew that you had a crush on

Wayne, and that Wayne had a crush on you, so I simply tried to help things along. Honest! I didn't mean any harm . . ."

Katy had started to laugh.

"But even though I tried to pull some strings, it didn't work out! So tell me: How did you two ever get together?"

"Simple," Katy said with a shrug. "*I* invited *him* to the dance!"

Chris and Susan both burst out laughing.

"Good for you!" exclaimed Susan. "See, Chris, Katy and Wayne didn't need you to play matchmaker after all!"

"Aw, gee, Sooz. I was only trying to help!"

After Wayne delivered Chris's doughnut, he whisked Katy away once again.

"Sorry to monopolize her," he apologized with a bashful grin. "But, well, Katy and I have a lot to talk about!"

Chris just sighed. "So much for my matchmaking abilities!"

"Hey," said Bob, "instead of worrying about your friend's date, how about me? I'm beginning to feel neglected!"

"Once the band gets back from its break, you won't have a chance to!" Chris returned. "Don't forget that you've already promised to dance every single dance with me, for the entire evening!"

"Sounds good to me!"

"But in the meantime, Bob and Bill," she went on, "there's something I want to tell you both about."

"What's that?"

"It's a theory I developed," Chris said with mock seriousness. "It has to do with autumn, and Halloween, and pumpkins . . ."

138

"Oh, no!" Susan groaned. "Not the Pumpkin Principle!"

"Exactly," her twin replied calmly. "Because I'm beginning to believe that I've really stumbled on to something!"

Susan just grimaced, rolling her eyes upward.

But Bill and Bob seemed interested.

"The Pumpkin Principle, huh?" said Bill. "It sounds fascinating. I can't wait to hear all about it!"

"Me, too," his twin agreed. "Maybe at Fozzy's later on? Over ice cream sodas?"

"*Now* you're talking!" Susan chuckled. "Even *I'll* agree to that! But for now, I see that the band is setting up once again. And all I want to do is *dance*!"

Neither Chris nor Bob nor Bill needed a second invitation.

ABOUT THE AUTHOR

Cynthia Blair grew up on Long Island, earned her B.A. from Bryn Mawr College in Pennsylvania, and went on to get a M.S. in marketing from M.I.T. She worked as a marketing manager for food companies but now has abandoned the corporate life in order to write.

She lives on Long Island with her husband, Richard Smith, and their son Jesse.